IT WILL

ALWAYS

BE US

I0689722

THERESA SEDERHOLT

It Will Always Be Us: A Fitz Series
Copyright © 2018 by Theresa Sederholt

ISBN: ISBN: 978-0-9976692-8-2

All rights reserved. This book or any portion thereof may not be reproduced or used in any manner whatsoever without the express written permission of the publisher except for the use of brief quotations in the book review.

The author acknowledges the copyrighted or trademarked status and trademark owners of the following word marks mentioned in this work of fiction: InStyle magazine. Cork and Kerry in Rockville Centre. Tugboat. Dick Tracey decoder ring. Starbucks. NYPD Blue. Blue Bloods. Discovery Channel and National Geographic. Big Bang Theory. David Garrett playing "Stairway to Heaven." "Perfect" by Ed Sheeran with Andrea Bocelli. MacBook pro. "My Girl" by Dylan Scott. Cinnabons. Enigma Typewriter. The Godfather, "Keep your friends close and your enemies closer." Hello Kitty. Chris Young's "Who I Am with You." "Broken Halos" by Chris Stapleton. Ed Sheeran's "Thinking Out Loud." Hillman Spike Concrete Anchors. Ristorante Da Claudio.

This is a work of fiction. Names, characters, businesses, places, events, and incidents are either the products of the author's imagination or used in a fictitious manner. Any resemblance to actual persons, living or dead, or actual events is purely coincidental.

This book contains strong language, graphic sexual situations, and violence. It is not intended for anyone under the age of 18.

Publisher: Theresa Sederholt ©
Cover designer, formatter and all around goddess: Stacey Ryan Blake, Champagne Book Design.
Editor: Jacquelyn Ayres.
Photographer: David Wills

Francine

You were my first friend, and you will always be my best friend. You are the person I know I can always count on. You've made me laugh and, yes, you've made me cry. Your strength and support has gotten me through so much in life. Being sisters keeps our childhood alive forever. I'm truly blessed that we will always have each other.

Love you always

You are my calm
When the chaos begins
And everything starts
To spiral out of control
I reach out my hand
And have no fear
That yours is already there
Waiting to take mine.

~Julie Mishler

IT WILL *ALWAYS* BE US

CHAPTER ONE

Bailey Davis

I<small>T's</small> <small>TIME</small> I <small>BEGIN</small> <small>TO</small> make some order out of Emerson's finances. He's been dead almost three months, yet, it seems more like
three years. Every day without him feels like a lifetime. People
die everyday, that's a fact. Yet, how many leave a huge cluster-fuck
for their surviving family to figure out? I venture to say—more than
anyone cares to admit. But, then again, what the hell do I know?
Emerson and I had a deal; he took care of all the finances, and I never had to worry if the mortgage was paid or if the electric was going to get shut off. I took care of the maintenance inside the house,
along with our three kids, Ella who is fifteen, Lilly who is thirteen,
and Collin who is ten. Add to that a bat-shit crazy dog named Sad
Sack, Jett, the five-year-old goldfish that never seems to die, and
Diamond Jim, the turtle, and my life is one hell of a daily organized
mess. A chaotic mess at best, but I don't mind it. I knew what I
signed up for, and I never had any regrets. Not too many people can
say that, at least the people I know.

What I never expected was for my husband to up and drop dead in the middle of delivering his closing argument during the biggest case of his entire career. It was a case he took pro bono. Those are the ones that meant the most to him. On a good note, Emerson won the case. On a bad note, he'll never know it.

Friends. I thought I had so many. What a fucking joke. No one wants a young widow hanging around their husband. In my neck of Brookville, Long Island, most of these wives are the second go-round, at least that's what I've seen. The first wife supports the family while the husband goes to school or starts his business. When the husband finally makes it, the wife thinks she's paid her dues; now it's time to reap the rewards. Unfortunately for the wife, that's when the husband dumps her for a trophy wife. Lucky for me, Emerson always said when he married me, he married up. We were as close as two people could be.

We met while he was still in law school. It was fashion week in New York. He was working as a security guard. I was just coming off of my first international cover. It was the first time I was requested by a top designer to wear his exclusive line on the Catwalk. That's when I knew I had made it. It's also where Emerson swept me off my feet. Before I knew it, we were getting married. I continued to model while he finished school. Law school is very expensive. He still had to take out student loans to help pay for it, and he reassured me they didn't have to be paid back until he started working. We used my modeling for all the bills, which made life much easier for us. Emerson was able to concentrate on his studies; no more part time jobs.

We were just starting out, the two of us in a small one bedroom basement apartment in Dyker Heights, Brooklyn. We had what we needed and not much more. We were young but we grew into the comfortable marriage we have today. Well . . . had. Now I'm left here, picking up the pieces.

Here I am, sitting in a house that is right around *five thousand* square feet, in front of a mountain of bills, and I have no idea which end is up. Fortunately, my best friend Roslyn is a financial advisor and has offered to help me make some sense of all of it. Her husband Jake worked with Emerson at the District Attorney's Office. That is until Jake became the head prosecutor and Emerson decided to go out on his own. He was aiming to be the top divorce attorney in New York. I could never understand why he would want to surround himself with misery. He claimed it kept everything in perspective for him.

I head into the kitchen, taking stock along the way. So much stuff. To me, that's all it ever was—*stuff*. To Emerson, it meant he arrived. To me, it means nothing, and no matter how much I preach to my kids that it means nothing, they have come to expect *this* lifestyle. Sad Sack's barking snaps me out of my daydream; Ro is here.

She comes in like a whirlwind. Never a hair out of place. Always dressed to the nines. She even looks like that running to the supermarket. Me—yoga pants with no holes and an oversized t-shirt and I'm golden.

"I just put up a pot of coffee, do you want a cup?" I'm already pulling a cup out of the cabinet for her since I know coffee is her weakness.

"Of course. Were you able to find all of Emerson's papers?"

I cringe knowing she's not going to like my answer. "There are stacks all over his home office along with a mountain of bills. I haven't gone through anything in his office yet, but his paralegal, Ruby, has already boxed everything up for me. It's just a matter of speaking to the landlord and removing all of the boxes. I figured I could swing by later in the week."

She cradles her cup in both hands, takes a sip of God's nectar, and I could swear she hummed. "Well, then we better get started."

As we head down the hall toward the office, I take a deep breath and prepare myself for the next hurdle. I open the door and step aside to let her take it all in.

"Bailey, you can't be serious. Your entire house is spotless. There is never a thing out of place. This room looks like someone threw a stick of dynamite in here."

"I actually organized it a little bit for you. The first stack is the bills. The other six stacks are things I know nothing about." I wave my hand over them as if they will magically disappear, just like my husband did.

"Leave me alone in here, so I can think clearly. Just make sure you keep the coffee coming." She heads further into the room, takes off her shoes, and rolls up her sleeves. I don't get to ask her anything. She shoos me away as Sad Sack curls up under the desk . . . traitor.

I leave her alone and head back to the kitchen to refresh my coffee before I head out back to the deck. Ella left a stack of fashion magazines on the coffee table. Flipping through this month's latest issue of *InStyle* magazine makes me feel like I'm seventy instead of forty-two years old. Ella wants to break into the fashion business so badly, but her father always said no. I'm sure now that he's gone, she'll be hitting me up to try it. If only it was as easy as she thinks it is. Nowadays, life seems to be filled with a lot of if onlies. I close my eyes and listen to the distant sound of the wind chime. I bought it on our honeymoon. I love all the different colors and the light sounds it makes when there is a gentle breeze. Emerson hated it, but he would never tell me no. I think this is the most relaxed I've been in three months. Probably because Ro is worrying about the financial mess and not me.

"Bailey!"

I jump up at the sound of my name, knocking over my empty coffee cup. Sad Sack comes running to see if there is any food involved.

"Ro, you nearly scared me to death."

"I've been calling you for the last ten minutes. I'm ready to go over everything with you."

Sad Sack climbs on the lounge chair and growls at the pillow, seemingly having no intention on coming inside. I follow her inside, mentally preparing myself for the worst. When I step inside the office, I'm in shock. The stack of bills is still the same but the six other stacks have been reduced down to two. I can even see the top of the desk!

"So, how does it look?"

"Do you want the good news first or the bad news?"

"I'm not in the mood for games, Ro. Either way, you'll be giving me both, so just tell me everything."

"Okay, there are two stacks. The first one consists of anything in Emerson's name that could be discharged or forgiven with a death certificate. In the second stack, there are things that you both had jointly. Those are not forgiven. He died and you assume responsibility for the balances. He did have an insurance policy specifically for the student loans. After breaking it down as to what you can write off and what you have to pay, taking into account the insurance policy, you are left with twenty-five thousand dollars."

"Oh, so at least I'll have some money after all of that."

She takes my hands and holds them tightly in hers. Her face is etched with sadness. "No, Bailey, that's what you will still owe."

I sink into the sofa and she sits next to me. I'm trying to be brave and process it all. "How could that be? He made a lot of money."

"And he spent a lot of money. This house alone was just under two million. The kids' tuition is insane. All three kids' tuitions combined is costing you ninety-six thousand a year, and that's without any extra curricular activities!"

"What about life insurance and his investments, surely that covers a lot of this." My hands are shaking and I feel a bad case of the hives coming on.

"He leveraged everything he had to open his own practice. The business was just starting to show a profit but not enough to pay off any of the debt he incurred. You know rule of thumb is that the first three years in business are usually a loss. All the years in business, Emerson never showed a profit. I did find papers from an attorney. Apparently, he set up a revocable trust. I'm not sure what's in it. Thankfully it's not an irrevocable trust, otherwise, nothing could be moved out of it. All I found is the receipt from the lawyer's office. The only thing the receipt says is *set up of revocable trust*. It might not even exist anymore, especially if he was in this much debt. I don't know an easy way to put this; Bailey, you're broke. The best thing you can do is have an estate sale. Put the kids in public school, sell this house, and get a job."

Her words are sinking in, and my stomach is in knots. "You make it sound so easy. I wouldn't even know where to begin."

"Don't worry. Lucky for you, I have a ton of friends that specialize in everything you'll need done. I'll make some calls this afternoon and get the ball rolling. Now, as far as his IRA, you are the beneficiary. I can set up a transfer of the IRA into an inherited IRA. Since you're a widow and under the age of fifty-nine and a half, you can access the money without paying the ten percent penalty. Depending upon market value, you could end up with about two-hundred-fifty thousand dollars. You will be taxed on it, but at this point, it's a matter of survival."

"Can I use some of the IRA money to pay off the student loans that I'm responsible for?"

"You could, but the interest rate is very low, so you might not want to use up all your capital. Let the dust settle before you do anything like that. Down the road, if that's what you want to do, we can do that. You have a lot of equity in this house. If you sell, you can roll that into a more affordable house."

The thought of the repo man coming to my house in the middle of the night sends a chill up my spine. "How long do I have before things get bad?"

"By bad I'm assuming you mean creditors harassing you and your cars being repossessed, that sort of thing. I would say thirty days tops. I mean, you really haven't paid one bill in three months. I went through all your outstanding bills and prioritized them. You have until noon tomorrow to pay the electric bill, after that they are shutting it off."

"I have some money in my checking account. I could probably pay that one." I go to the desk and look at the bill. It's close to five thousand dollars! "How the hell could electric cost so much?"

"This is a huge house, Bailey. Emerson had you on the payment plan. You pay the same amount every month. In the end, it's supposed to balance out. They haven't bothered you because you had a credit from last year. They used that up and that's your past due balance. How much do you have in your checking account?"

I'm staring at her like she has three heads. How did I ever let myself get into this mess? "I might have two grand, but that's everything."

"Look, I'll pay the electric bill for you. Eventually, you'll be in a position to pay me back. You pay the water bill, that's more do-able for you. The first thing you need to do today is go down to Social Security with the death certificate. You'll get a small amount monthly until each kid is sixteen. The kids themselves will collect monthly until they are eighteen."

I'm trying to absorb everything she's saying, but I can't believe my husband would leave us in such a mess. "My children; I can't possibly tell them what's going on. Ro, you need to keep this be-tween us—please," I plead with her.

She takes both my hands and gives me a reassuring squeeze. "Okay, but eventually they will find out. They're not idiots. There's only so long you can hide this from them." She lets go of my hands, bends down and picks up her purse. She's going to leave and, for the first time, I'm feeling panicked at the thought of being home alone. "Look, I've got to go. I'll handle the electric bill when I get to work. You need to get started on this right away."

I watch her walk out the door. Feeling overwhelmed by the magnitude of loss I'm now going through, I pick up the picture of my husband and I on his desk. I run my fingers over his smile. They were happy times. He always made me laugh. Now, all I want to do is cry.

CHAPTER TWO

I SPENT A WHOLE WEEK dealing with all of Emerson's stuff. Everything from donating all of his suits to closing down his office. Some people were very nice, like the landlord for his office; he broke the lease and didn't charge me. On the other side of that coin was the leasing company for his car. I swear if I could have reached through the phone and kicked the guy in his nuts, I would have. No matter how many times I told him that my husband was dead, he kept trying to put the balance of the lease in my name. In the end, he sent someone down to pick up the car, along with a notarized copy of the death certificate.

I'm doing everything I possibly can not to disrupt my kids' lives. I know Ro said to pull them out of private school but I can't do it, not just yet. The bell ringing, along with the dog barking, snaps me out of my pity party. I open the door, and Ro comes in like a whirlwind.

"What are you doing here? Did we have a meeting set up?"

"Thanks, Bailey, it's nice to see you too. I wanted to find out how much progress you made and if there is anything you need me to help you with."

We head into the kitchen and I pour us each a cup of coffee. "I decided today to bring my jewelry to the pawn shop two towns over."

"Are you afraid you might see someone you know?"

"Of course it's embarrassing, but, Ro, what's more embarrassing is my kids' friends finding out. You know how cruel kids can be." I'm watching her run her fingertip round and round her coffee cup. It's hypnotizing as I sit here, wondering what is going through her mind.

"Have you thought about going back to work? I mean you're still beautiful."

"Thanks, but I'm too old. In the fashion world, I'm considered a relic. Besides, after three kids, all my assets are falling down. Kind of like that kids' song 'London Bridge is Falling Down.'"

"Sometimes your thinking is so warped. What about being an agent? Hell, Ella is beautiful, and she's busting to get into the business. What could it hurt?"

"I thought about it for a hot minute. The devil on my left shoulder told me to do it, to give the kid her shot. The angel on my right shoulder reminded me what the life of a fashion model is really all about. In the end, I'm not going to pimp my kid out, no matter how desperate I get."

I pour some more coffee while Ro continues staring out the window, watching Sad Sack chase the birds. "You know, Ro, if he ever caught one of those birds, he wouldn't know what to do with it. Kind of like all of us, chasing after a dream, and if we get it, then what?"

She has a melancholy look. I doubt it has anything to do with the dog. "At least he's consistent."

Sad Sack gives up the chase and comes through the doggie door. He runs right up to Ro and nearly knocks her over.

"Bailey, he's a beast."

"Only with you."

"Do you want me to go with you to the pawn shops?"

"No reason for both of us to be embarrassed."

She steps closer to me and pulls me into a much-needed hug. "Hey, look at me; there is nothing to be embarrassed about. You're doing what ever you have to do to keep your family together and a roof over their heads. Your kids are your world, as they should be." I know she's right but I'm still finding all of this very difficult.

"Bailey, what happened with the trust we found?"

"I have an appointment with the lawyer next week. And before you ask, he was on vacation and that was the soonest they could fit me in. Look, I better get going. I want to be back home when the kids get here."

"Okay, why don't I call the girls and see if we can get together for cocktails tonight?"

"I have no money. Remember, I'm the one who is selling off all my personal stuff to the pawn shop."

She rolls her eyes at my sarcasm. "I'll pay, wiseass. I think you could use a mental break. Besides, Gail is going away and it will be a nice send off for her."

"Where is she going?"

"I'll let her explain it all to you."

I pass her two of my fur coats. With my arms full, we head into the garage to load up my car. "Jeez, woman, how many furs do you have?"

"If you must know, four too many. I hate them, but Emerson thought otherwise. The furrier offered to come to the house, but that's the last thing I want. I don't want my kids to know what is going on, at least not yet."

I finish loading everything. I know I have to get going but dread is making me procrastinate. "Look, I'll meet you at Cork and Kerry in Rockville Centre at nine. I can't stay long, but by the time I'm done today, I know I will need a drink."

"Great! Now knock 'em dead. I'll see you later." She sashays off, seemingly excited about tonight. A lot more excited then what I'm about to do.

First up—the furrier.

Selling off everything of value I own just to keep up pretenses was the most humiliating thing I've had to do in a long time. Right now, I hate my husband. I've never hated anyone, but how could he leave me in this fucked up mess? I'm sitting at his desk with our wedding picture clutched tightly in my hands. How the hell did so much change right under my nose. I know he didn't ask to die, but he should have been more responsible with us. Maybe it's the stages of grief that is making me feel this way. Maybe (*realistically*) I'm just as much to blame. I mean, I should have paid more attention to what the hell was happening around me. Then again, there is a level of trust with your spouse. You're supposed to be in the same canoe, paddling in sync. After today, I realize I have no choice; I have to sell the house. There is no way I can keep up the payments, along with everything else it entails. Even if I try, I'm doing the same damn thing Emerson did, living a lie. I just don't know what to tell my children.

I'm not home more than five minutes when I hear the kids at the door. Lucky for me, one of the other parents picked up my carpool week. But come Monday, I need to have a better plan. A plan that doesn't include these constant pity parties. I put on my brave face, put the picture back on the desk, and get up to go face the music. When I do, my knee whacks the side of the desk and the picture falls, shattering the glass. "*Damn it!*" Thankfully, all the glass stayed within the frame. I hold it over the trash and carefully let all the pieces fall in. When I pull the picture out, a piece of paper comes out with it. I have no idea what it is, just some random numbers.

"*What the hell?*"

"Mom, are you okay? I've been calling out your name. Why are you just standing here, staring at that piece of paper?"

"Sorry, I didn't hear you. I only got home a few minutes before you did, Ella." I quickly shove the paper in my back pocket.

"I'm not an idiot, Mom; what's on the paper?"

"More stuff of your father's that I'm trying to deal with. It's nothing for you to concern yourself with. How was school today?" I gently place my hand on her back and guide her out of the office. I don't need her to take notice of the stack of past due notices sitting out in the open on the desk.

"It sucked, as usual. I feel like everyone is walking on eggshells around me. My fifteen minutes of fame was my dad dying on television. I wish everyone would just move on already."

"What about Nikki? I mean, for Christ's sake, she's your best friend."

"She's the one who told me that they are afraid to say anything to me. They don't want me to have a melt down or something. God forbid I should embarrass them."

She is the strong one. The one that everyone comes to when they need that shoulder to cry on. I hear her late at night, when she thinks I'm sleeping; I hear her crying. My heart breaks for her. I take her hand and stop her before we get into the kitchen with the rest of the kids. "El, I know you already said no, but please reconsider counseling." I get the standard eye roll along with a *what the fuck is wrong with you?* look. "Just promise you'll think about it."

"Yes, I promise. Happy now?"

She heads into the kitchen in front of me. The chaos for snacks is already underway. I'm standing in the doorway, feeling my heart in my throat as I work up the courage to tell them the truth. Our life is going to change drastically, yet again.

"Mom, why are you just standing there?" Collin shouts out with a mouth full of a chocolate chip cookie.

Lilly puts her hand up in front of his mouth and scrunches her face as if she smelled a skunk. "Collin, you're disgusting. Mom, can't you teach your son some manners?" She's my miss prim and proper. She's nothing like any of us . . . not sure whose child she is.

"Collin, your sister is right. Close your mouth when you have food in it."

He rolls his eyes and pops another piece of his cookie in his mouth. "Weirdo. At least I eat my cookies like a normal person. Unlike you who uses a fork and a soup bowl."

"I'm not a weirdo. I told you before; I don't want to make a mess and this way the entire cookie gets soaked in the milk."

"Like I said—weirdo."

They keep bickering back and forth while El is glued to her phone.

"Okay, I need everyone's attention, that includes you too, El." I take a deep breath and now all eyes on me. "Since your father's death, I've been going through our financial situation. I'm not going to bore you with the details. However, we are going to have to sell this house. There is no way I can keep up with the payments and maintenance."

El's eyes grow wide and tears dance along her bottom lashes. "Mom, does that mean we have to change schools? I only have two years left here; please don't do this to me."

"I'm sorry. We just can't afford the tuition along with all the other expenses. My goal is to keep a roof over our heads and food on the table."

She grabs her phone, jumps up and runs out of the kitchen.

Lilly is staring at me, not uttering a word. Collin gets up and puts his glass in the sink before coming back and giving me a kiss on the cheek.

"As long as I can still hang with my friends, I'm cool with it. I've got to do my homework."

He leaves and now it's just Lilly and me. She might be only thirteen but she's an old soul. "You're very quiet; what are your thoughts?"

"What are my thoughts?! Does it really matter?"

I'm taken aback by her tone, so unlike her. "Of course it matters. I'm not doing this to make everyone miserable—trust me—I'm miserable enough for all of us. I'm trying to figure out how to keep it all together." I have to remember even though she acts like an old lady in a young girl's body, she is still only thirteen.

"Didn't Daddy have insurance?"

"Unfortunately, not enough."

"Well, I guess we have no choice. Do what you have to. I only hope you don't become as irresponsible as he was."

She gets up, puts her bowl and fork in the dishwasher and walks out, with Sad Sack following closely behind her. She's the one I worry the most about. Ella is a fly-off-the-handle girl. At any given moment, you know exactly what she's thinking. Collin, he is the laid back kind of child. As long as he has his friends and his Lacrosse, he's happy. But Lilly, she turns it all inward. She always solves everything on her own, never asking for anything from any of us. But, this is not something she can deal with on her own. She's the main reason I brought the kids to counseling.

I glance up at the clock and if I don't head into the shower now, I'll be late meeting the girls for happy hour. Who knows, maybe they will have a better solution.

CHAPTER
THREE

I SHIMMY OUT OF MY jeans. I'm about to toss them down the laundry chute when I remember the paper I shoved into my pocket. I pull it out and examine it closer. It's a series of numbers, letters, and symbols. It's Emerson's handwriting but why hide this, and what is it? I grab my phone and take a picture of the paper before I shove it into my purse. Maybe one of the girls can help me figure it out. In the meantime, I need to get ready.

After a quick shower, I sit at my vanity and try to remember what it feels like to put some effort into my appearance. It seems like such a long time ago rather than the short three months. I feel like I've already lost a lifetime. I dab the corners of my eyes while fighting to hold back the dam that's about to burst. *"Come on, Bailey, you can do this."* I finish up and give myself the once-over before I head out the door. It's not about impressing anyone else; it's about believing in myself.

For once traffic was light and, on top of that, the parking gods were with me. It's a typical sized crowd for a Friday night at Cork and Kerry. Thankfully, Ro, Gail, and Regina are already here, and they've snagged a booth. As I make my way toward them, I force myself to put on a brave face. This is the first time we will all be together since the funeral. I knew Ro would come by to see me—if for nothing else—to help me with my financial stuff. I can understand Gail not coming by. She is the lead Medical Examiner for Kings County. Sadly, she is one of the busiest people I know. I don't think she gets more than four hours of sleep a night. But, I mean, Regina's daughter Megan and my Lilly are best friends. She even does the car pool nonsense, yet she's never stopped over. I asked Lilly if they seemed a little different since her dad died. All she did was shrug her shoulders and walk away.

I catch the waiter just as he's leaving the table and order a martini.

"Hey, sorry I'm late; time got away from me." Gail moves over and as I sit down, she pulls me into a much-needed hug. I know her concern is genuine, but she's usually a very reserved type of person, so I'm taken back by her affection.

"I'm sorry I haven't been around. How are you and the kids holding up?"

The waiter comes with my drink, giving me a minute to catch my breath. "We have good days and bad, but we are dealing."

"You know my schedule is always nuts, but if you need anything just ask—please."

Ro reaches over and gives my hand a squeeze. "Listen, Bailey, we've all been friends for a long time, so I brought them up to speed on everything."

If there was a hole big enough, I would crawl into it. I know Ro means well, but I'm not one to put my personal stuff out there. I hope she didn't tell them I'm selling off my jewelry and furs just to make ends meet. I try to down my martini, hoping for some liquid courage. But before I can finish, Regina holds up her glass for a toast.

"Here's to new beginnings. And if you decide to sell your house, Justin will help you with it."

I catch Gail roll her eyes, and I'm trying not to laugh. I'm surprised it took Regina this long to pitch her husband's real estate business.

"How about tonight we forget about all my troubles and have some fun?"

Everyone agrees and before to long my hardships take a back burner. Regina is filling us in on all the local gossip that she found out from her Yoga class. While Ro fills us in on her husband Jake's latest big win at the Manhattan District Attorney's office.

I'm listening to her, but my mind is on that piece of paper I found today. I was intent on discussing it with the girls tonight but my gut is telling me not to. I could share it with Jake. After all, he is one of Emerson's oldest friends. Then again, if it were something bad, it would be another thing my kids would have to deal with. Maybe I'll wait and share it with Gail. She's very logical and level-headed. Regina and Ro get up and head to the ladies room. I'll never understand why women need to go in pairs. I go when I have to go, not when everyone says it's time.

Now with Ro and Regina out of the picture, it's the perfect opportunity to show it to Gail. "Hey, I want to show you something. But please, keep this just between us."

"Of course, is something wrong?"

I fish the piece of paper out of my bag and pass it to her. "I found this hidden in Emerson's office."

"What do you mean by hidden?"

"It was behind a picture of Emerson and me that was on his desk. I dropped the picture, and it broke. When I picked up the pieces, that paper came out. I venture to say by the hiding spot that he didn't want me to know about it, or anyone for that matter. The problem is I have no idea what *it* is."

She is staring at the paper, running her finger over the writing. "Yeah, by that hiding spot, it's safe to say he didn't want you to know about it. Unfortunately, I have no idea what it is. There are too many numbers, letters, and special characters for it to be a bank account. If you want, I can have my friend Fitz look into it for you. He's a retired cop and is now a partner at The Cooper Agency. They do PI work along with security and a slew of other stuff. "

"Do you trust him? I mean of course you do if he's your friend, but if it's bad, I don't want my kids to know. I have to protect them, Gail; I'm all they have."

"I trust him with my life. The girls are coming back," she says and quickly passes the paper to me, but I push it back.

"I already have a copy of it. Have your friend look into it and let me know what he says. Thank you."

She puts the paper into her bag and the girls are back followed by two guys that look like they stepped off the pages of a high-end fashion magazine.

"Gail, Bailey, we found these nice single guys all by themselves at the bar, Robert and Chester." Regina's words come out slurred. I catch Gail rolling her eyes again and I let out a little chuckle.

Gail and I look at each other and then back at the guys. Before I can stop myself, I blurt out, "Chester!?"

He sits in the booth next to me. "Yes, it's a family name. If nothing else, it gets women talking to me."

"Yet, you're still single." Again, no filter. Maybe it's the martini talking.

"Are you single?"

I feel my heart sink a little and my eyes pool with unshed tears. Before I can answer, Ro leans in close to him. "She's recently widowed. This is her first night out, so go easy."

Now, I'm pissed. "Ro, everyone does not need to know all my business!"

He takes my hand and gives it a soft squeeze. "I'm sorry for your loss."

He gets up and just like that, he leaves with Robert following.

"Well, that was a great mood breaker. Look, Ro, I don't want my life broadcasted out there for the whole world to hear. I came here tonight to forget about everything. All I want is to have a little fun. I'm not out here trying to find a man."

Regina leans on the table no doubt trying to steady herself. "Listen, Bailey, maybe you should be looking for a man. Hell, yours left you high and dry. You're not getting any younger, and if you want to keep the lifestyle that you and your children have come to expect, then maybe you need to put your feelings aside and concentrate on what's in front of you."

"So, what am I supposed to do, Regina, spread my legs for any man that will have me? Of course, that's only after I've checked his bank account to make sure there are the appropriate number of zeros." I get up and toss some cash on the table. She grabs my arm stopping me from leaving.

"Emerson did what ever he had to do to give his kids everything. Maybe you could learn from that."

I reach back to slap her, but Gail grabs my arm. "She's drunk, and it's not worth it. Let's go, I'm sure she won't even remember any of this in the morning."

We head out, leaving Ro to deal with Regina. The cool night air hits me, along with the realization that maybe Regina was right. After all, I'm a mother and, no matter what, I will always put my children before me.

"Gail, where are you parked?"

"I didn't drive; Ro picked me up."

"Come on, hop in. I'll take you home." I'm quiet for a bit, driving mindlessly on Sunrise Highway. "Tell me more about your friend," I inquire.

"What do you want to know?"

"What makes you think he can help me?"

"When it comes to a puzzle, he's like a dog with a bone. I've known him for seventeen years and he's never given up, ever."

At the red light, I glance her way. I notice she's got a melancholy look on her face. I wonder if it has to do with her friend? The honking horn alerts me that the light has changed. I don't want to pry, but maybe she needs talk about him. "Are you and he, you know . . ."

"No, Fitz and I are friends."

"You're quick to cut me off. Would you like it to be more?"

She becomes very quiet and turns her head toward the window so I can't see her face. However, she can't hide the tear she wipes from her cheek.

"Gail, you know you can tell me anything; I would never betray your confidence."

"He makes it easy for women to want to love him. Unfortunately, when I finally got up the nerve to tell him how I felt about him, he had proposed to the only girl he ever wanted. They're happy. They have a child, and she is a really great person. Even if I wanted to hate her, I couldn't. He's living his dream and I'm happy for him. Not everyone gets to live the life they dreamed about. Sometimes, all we have are fleeting moments that our heart captures like a photograph."

"That's so sad. Maybe if he knew how you felt, things would have been different."

I can hear her let out a deep breath and I realize how hard this must be for her to talk about.

"The day I decided to tell him how I felt was the day he proposed to MJ. He's only ever wanted her and she's only ever wanted him. Some things are just not to be."

"I'm sorry I wasn't there for you."

"You've been busy raising three great kids. I understand. Besides, there's nothing anyone could have done to change it."

"Doesn't matter; I still feel like a shitty friend."

I pull into her driveway, and all of the motion lights come on. There has to be at least a dozen of them. "Whoa, think you've got enough lights?"

"When I bought the house, Fitz put them up. I always thought he was a little over-the-top when it came to safety. However, nowadays, you can't take any chances. I'll talk to him about that paper and let you know what happens."

"Thank you," I say as she gets out and shuts the door. I watch to make sure she gets in okay and then head home.

CHAPTER FOUR

Fitz

Saturday is usually my day to work on my honey-do-list that MJ always seems to have for me. Except today, I was able to ditch the list after I got a call from Gail. I told her to come by the house, but she wanted privacy. Saturdays at the office are always busy, so we are meeting at Tugboat, a local coffee house, which is the halfway point for both of us. I don't mind; it gives me the opportunity to take Wanda out for a drive. I'm early, so I grab a table in the back and people watch. I don't have to wait long before she shows up.

"Hey, stranger." I get up and give her a big hug.

"Me? Just because you're no longer with the department doesn't mean you can't come by and pester me."

"I know. I've been really busy. Who knew I would be this busy after I retired? You sounded vague on the phone. Are you okay? What's going on?"

Before she can answer the waitress comes over to take our order. After she leaves, Gail takes a piece of paper out of her purse and passes it to me. While I stare at it, she fills me in on her friend Bailey and her husband Emerson.

"Who else knows about this piece of paper?"

"As far as I know, only Bailey and me."

"Good—keep it that way. I don't know what it is but give me a few days and let me see what I can find out. Do you think it's odd that he hid it from her?"

"Apparently, he hid a lot of things from her."

Before I can question her further, the waitress interrupts us with our food. I watch Gail move her food around her dish so nothing touches and I can't help but laugh at her quirkiness.

"So, back to Bailey; did she say what else he hid from her?"

"He put them into large financial debt, which Bailey knew nothing about."

I nearly choke on my food. "Wow, I can't imagine doing that to MJ. Not that I could get anything past her or would I want to. That's got to tell you something about their relationship. Maybe things weren't so rosy."

"I only know what I've seen. When they were together, they seemed happy. Their kids seem well-adjusted. But, who knows what goes on behind closed doors."

"Tell me more about him."

"He was originally with the DA's office. He left to go out on his own. His focus was divorce law. Like so many other lawyers, he did a lot of pro bono work, but he seemed to do more than his fair share. He was really making a name for himself out on the island. Then, out of nowhere, he died in the middle of his closing argument. He was young, Fitz—early forties—too young."

"When someone dies at a young age, it's even harder. Was it really a heart attack that killed him?"

She becomes very quiet, like someone who is searching for the right words. "I knew you would ask me that, so I pulled his autopsy report. I recused myself from doing the autopsy, since I knew him personally." She reaches into her bag and pulls out the report. Before she passes it to me, she squeezes my hand. "I can get into trouble sharing this with you."

She's always been a by the book person and I would never want her to compromise her beliefs because of me. I push it back towards her. "I don't need to see it. All I need is your word that it was really a heart attack."

"Thank you. It was what's usually referred to as the widow maker." She barely whispers as she shoves the paper back in her bag.

"So, let's go over what we do know. He was doing well, yet he was in debt. He hid stuff from his wife, including that piece of paper. What do you think he was into?"

"He wasn't selling drugs, otherwise he would not have been in so much debt. If he was doing drugs, it would have showed up in the toxicology report. Whatever he was doing, he wasn't very good at it, otherwise, they wouldn't be broke."

"Okay, give me a few days and I'll let you know what I come up with. Now enough of this, I feel like it's been forever since I've seen you. What's going on in your life?"

"I'm not going to be around for about two weeks. I finally took your advice and decided to go on the vacation of a lifetime. Well, at least for me it is. I'm going to Paris!"

"Wow, that's exciting. What made you decide on Paris?"

"Don't laugh; I closed my eyes and threw a dart at the map."

"And it just landed on Paris?"

"Well, it did take three tries to even hit the map, but I'm very excited."

"Who are you going with?"

"Myself. I want to travel before I'm too old to enjoy it."

I don't like the idea that she will be traveling to another country by herself. Not in the times we're living in. "Maybe you shouldn't be taking my advice. Does it have to be by yourself?"

"Fitz, I'll be fine. Besides, there is no one in my life right now. If I put it off until I find someone, it could be too late for me. Aren't you the one who is always saying you never want to wonder *what if?*"

"Like I said, maybe you shouldn't always listen to me. I know, how about joining one of those dating sites? Nowadays, it seems there are so many of them."

Her eyes grow wide and she nearly chokes on her coffee. "I'm sure they're great for some people, but after that case with the serial rapist on that dating site last year . . . I don't think I'll be going near any of them anytime soon. Don't worry, I'm a big girl and I can take care of myself. Besides, I realized a while ago that not everyone finds a cover for their pot."

"That only applies if you're giving up. Are you giving up?"

"No, Fitz, I'm being realistic. Most of my workdays are very long. I'm either working on someone or doing paperwork. By the time I get home, I'm either busy doing stuff around the house or too tired to do anything more then eat and decompress from the day. Hell, I don't even have time for a pet! How pathetic is that?"

I hate seeing her like this, there has to be something I can do to fix this. "What about an Iguana? I bet they aren't a lot of work." Her eyes grow wide and she bites her bottom lip. I can't tell if she's trying not to laugh or cry.

"An Iguana? Can I put a leash on it and walk it around the neighborhood?" She begins to laugh and I can't help but laugh along with her.

"Okay, maybe not an Iguana. Let's table the pet stuff for now. When you send me Bailey's contact information, include your itinerary—please."

"You know by nature I'm a cautious person, so what are you so worried about?"

"And you know by now that I'm a worry wart, so why can't you just do it and let me have a little peace of mind knowing I can find you?"

She slams her hand down and it rattles her cup. I think I hit a nerve.

"You are a stubborn man and I have no idea how the hell MJ deals with you."

"That's why I thank God every day for her and all my friends and family. Speaking of which, let me show you some new pictures of Patrick and Stella."

Like a typical father, I pull up a folder on my phone and pass it to her. As she flips through the photos, she seems so melancholy. "Gail, are you okay? You seem sad."

"I'm fine, Fitz. I can't believe how big Patrick is getting. He looks just like MJ. How is Stella doing?"

"She's an angel. She and Andy have really bonded. He makes sure she never forgets her mom. She has given Andy purpose, which is something he didn't have before. It's like they were meant to be together."

"What about her grandfather? Does she have any kind of relationship with him?"

The thought of that man puts a knot in my gut. "He wants nothing to do with her. Which for Stella, is for the best. Having him permanently removed from her life keeps her safe," I digress. She passes me back my phone, but I can't seem to shake the feeling that something is bothering her. "Are you sure nothing is wrong?"

"Yes, I'm sure. But, if I don't leave now, I'll never get everything done before I have to leave for vacation. I'll text you Bailey's contact information, along with my travel plans. Let me know what happens with that paper."

She gets up to leave and I get up and pull her into a hug. "I'll let you know what happens. Be safe and have a good time."

She heads out the door but not before she stops and waves. I can't seem to shake the dread that I'm feeling. I pull out the paper and stare at it for a while. I love a good puzzle, but I have no clue what this could possibly be. I do know someone who might be able to decipher it.

Me: Hey, got something I need you to look at.

Travis: Hello to you too. What've you got?

I snap a picture of the paper and send it to him.

Me: Gail asked me to look into this for a friend. Not sure what it is.

Travis: It's part of a string. Do you have the rest of it?

Me: That's all I have.

Travis: You need to find the rest of it.

Me: I can't find something if I don't know what it is.

Travis: Like I said, it's part of a string code. The part you sent me would connect to another part and from there, I can decode it.

Me: Guess you don't have your Dick Tracey decoder ring. Where do you think I would find the rest of the code?

Travis: No, I don't have my decoder ring today. Seriously though, where did you find this code?

Me: The client's husband hid it behind a photo. Before you ask, he's dead. Natural causes.

Travis: Well, he must have had a good reason to hide it.

Me: How much more am I looking for?

Travis: I really can't say without knowing what it goes to.

Me: What do you mean goes to?

Travis: Just because it's part of a string of code doesn't mean it's for a computer program. Think of it like a broken key that you only found half of. Now you need to find the other half.

Keep hunting and let me know what happens. I'm here if you need me.

Me: Thanks.

My phone bings and it's the information from Gail. Before I contact Bailey, I need to head into the office. I've got to find out who Emerson Davis really was.

CHAPTER
FIVE

N<small>O MATTER WHAT TIME OF</small> day I head into work, I know Hudson will always be there. My parents took her in after everything she thought she knew to be true was a lie and her world fell apart. They did the same thing for me so many years ago. We are family by choice, and I couldn't ask for anything more. Someone asked me about her once, to which I replied, "she's like an old chair, always there and always a comfort." Unfortunately, she couldn't get past the old chair, and that earned me a punch in the gut. It took me a week of groveling and Starbucks coffee to make my way back into her good graces. She's on the phone when I enter, so I slip the coffee down in front of her.

Hudson's desk is always neat as a pin; mine always looks like mass chaos. I push everything aside and begin my internet search. The best way to find out the good, the bad, and the ugly on someone is a quick Google search. From there, I can decide which way I want to go. The first thing that pops up is the obituary for Emerson Davis. I wasn't expecting someone so young. He looks familiar but I can't place him. The obit is the usual fluff stuff.

"Hey, thanks for the coffee. Why are you here on a Saturday?"

"I'm looking into something for Gail." I'm reading about his career when Hudson rolls her chair behind me.

"Oh, that's the guy that dropped dead in the middle of his closing argument."

"How did you know that? Do you know him?"

"No, Pat and I watch the news together every morning before I walk Annie to church. It's our thing. Anyway, it was all over the news. He used to be with the district attorney's office in Manhattan. He left and went into divorce law. He only took top cases, and Long Island was filled with the rich and not-so-famous for him to choose from. He was working a pro bono case when it happened. My law professor also brought it up in class. Some of the students were wondering if there were grounds for an appeal since he dropped dead in court. You know . . . influencing the judge and the jury. But, I guess it wasn't a problem. So, why are you looking into him?"

I pull out the paper that Gail gave me and pass it to her as I fill her in on everything.

"So, she only found it by accident. Makes you wonder what else he was hiding."

"My thoughts exactly. I wouldn't dream of hiding anything from my wife," I admit. She throws her head back and laughs. "What?"

"The thought of you trying to hide something from MJ is hilarious."

She rolls herself back towards her desk. I pull up Gail's itinerary. She leaves for Paris in three days. Why couldn't the dart land in the United States? I need to shake off my uneasy feelings about her trip and focus on the case at hand. The first thing I need to do is meet with Bailey. I want to see where Emerson worked and lived. That might give me some sort of clue as to where I can find the rest of this key that Travis was talking about. While I dig around on the internet for more on Emerson, I call Bailey.

"Hi, Bailey, my name is Fitz. Gail asked me to look into the paper you found."

"Hi. Wow, that was really quick."

"Yeah, Gail hardly ever asks for anything, so when she calls, I know it's important to her. I'd like to discuss all of this with you in person. You know, see where he worked, and try to get to the bottom of this as quickly as possible for you. Are you available this afternoon?"

"I already closed up his office and brought everything to the house. My kids are in and out all day, so maybe we can meet when they are in school on Monday. I do have to see my husband's attorney in the morning for the reading of the will, but I'm free after that. Will that work for you?"

"Yes, whatever is convenient for you."

"Okay, in the meantime, I'll text you his assistant's number. Her name is Ruby Fox. I'll give her a heads up that you will be reaching out to her."

"That's fine, but please don't tell her about the paper."

"I won't say anything. Thanks for helping me with this."

"No problem. I'll see you on Monday."

She quickly sends me the text, along with another thank you. I can't imagine what she is going through, losing someone so young and then finding out he left behind secrets. I could never imagine life without MJ.

Maybe I'll have Hudson call Ruby first to break the ice. I look over and she has earbuds in and seems to be very engrossed in something on her computer. I'll just call myself.

She picked up on the first ring and agreed to meet me at a Starbucks near her home in Queens. Maybe I should take Hudson with me. She has a way of getting people to open up to her. I roll my chair over to her desk and pull out one of her earbuds.

"Hey, want to take a ride with me? I'm going to meet with

Emerson's assistant, Ruby."

"Where?"

"Queens."

"On Wanda?!"

"You know poor Wanda is going to get a complex."

"She is a frigging bike, Fitz."

She gets up and head towards the door and I'm right behind her laughing.

We pull up to the Starbucks and before we go inside Hudson pulls me toward her. "How do you want to play this?"

"I think you've been watching too many crime shows with dad. This is not an episode of *NYPD Blue*. It's just a conversation. I want her to feel comfortable enough that she'll freely talk about her boss."

"I was thinking more like *Blue Bloods*, but whatever." She throws her hands up, and we head inside. This time of day, the store is almost empty. There is a woman sitting alone near the counter. As we head toward her, she quickly stands up.

"Are you Fitz?"

"Yes, ma'am. You must be Ruby. This is my assistant, Hudson."

"You said on the phone that you wanted to talk about Emerson. I don't know what you think I could tell you, other than he had a heart attack."

I'm about to answer when I feel Hudson nudge my foot.

"Fitz said you were Emerson's assistant. I know for him to be as successful as he was, you were more than that. Let's face it, we do everything so our bosses can focus on one thing—winning."

"Girl, you got that right. I swear I had to do everything, even remind the man to eat."

"Fitz, I could use an iced tea, please. Ruby, would you like anything?"

"No, I'm good."

Hudson pulls her phone out of her bag, opens up the voice memo app and swipes it. "You can use my Starbucks app to pay." She attempts to pass it to me. I get what she's doing and push it back toward her.

"What kind of boss would I be if I made my wonderful assistant pay for her own drink?" I give her a smirk, which I'm sure I will pay for later. While I wait in line, I look over and noticed Hudson placed her phone down in front of her. Her privacy screen will make it impossible for Ruby to see the open app recording their conversation.

"Did you take care of his personal stuff too? You know like the banking and bills?"

"Of course, what's this all about?"

"He died so suddenly, I'm sure Bailey wants to make sure that she didn't miss anything. Did you know they were having some financial difficulty?"

"No way, I know for a fact they weren't. Money was running low but when I mentioned it to him, the next day he came in and gave me a check for fifty thousand dollars."

"Wow, did he do that a lot or was it a one time thing?"

"He did it whenever I needed it. Look, I don't know what's going on other than he was a great boss and now I'm out of a job."

"Like I said, we are just making sure nothing falls through the cracks. I'm sure Bailey wants to make sure that her three children are well taken care of."

"Well, if that's what she's worried about, she shouldn't. Emerson had a revocable trust that provided for all of his children."

"What do you mean by 'all of his children?'"

"He had another child, a daughter. He created a second trust for her. He wanted to keep her identity secret, but they are all provided for."

The line is long, and with Ruby's back toward me, I am able to hold back while I listen to most of what's being said. I slip back into the conversation at just the right moment. She seems to be defending him even after his death, why?

"Is the other woman aware that Emerson died?"

"Yes. It was a complicated situation; however, she is aware."

"Why do I feel like there is something you're not telling me?" Hudson reaches over and takes Ruby's hand. No doubt trying to reassure her that we are only here to help.

"Whatever you tell us will go no further, I promise."

She looks down, takes a deep breath and squeezes Hudson's hand. "He was a good man that made one really bad mistake. He was remorseful and ended it right away, but one day she showed up pregnant. I told him to demand a paternity test, but he just believed her. That was when he set up the second trust. The guilt ate away at him. I believe that's what killed him—guilt." She is ripping her napkin to shreds. Hudson takes Ruby's hand again, trying to offer some comfort.

"Who else knows about her? I can't imagine that he took this secret to his grave."

"No one knows because of who she is."

"Please, Ruby, at this point, keeping secrets is not going to help these children."

I'm hoping Hudson's plea doesn't fall on deaf ears.

"The woman was Bailey's friend, Regina Morris. The kids are friends and have no idea they are siblings. Do you understand that if this comes out, the ramifications would ruin so many lives?"

"Her friend, really?" Hudson squeaks out.

"Hudson, apparently, there is more to the story. I'm sure the man didn't set out to create such a mess." I forget sometimes that she can be naive.

"So, now maybe you can tell me the truth about where he was getting the money from." I press Ruby for more information while Hudson is still reeling from Emerson's betrayal. Ruby gathers up her bag and her trash. I think it's safe to say this interview is coming to a close. Maybe I pushed too hard, but I hate lies.

"I told you he never said anything to me as to where it was coming from. Now I need to go." She gets up and hurries out the door. Hudson and I are left to figure out this mess.

"Glad you recorded everything. It was not what I was expecting."

"Her friend, Fitz. What. The. Fuck. Is nothing sacred anymore?"

"When we get back to the office, I need you to pull everything you can on Regina Morris. I must get to Bailey before she meets with that attorney."

"How do you plan on doing that?"

"I'll figure it out. Let's get going."

We take off on Wanda, my mind replaying everything Ruby said. Coming up with fifty grand at the drop of a dime is not easy. Where the hell is the money coming from? I've got a bad feeling this is not going to end well.

CHAPTER
SIX

When we get back to the office, Sal is waiting . . . no doubt for Hudson. Sal is not just my business partner, he's also my friend. Hudson is like a little sister. I don't want to get crazy on them, but this could be a problem. For now, though, I'll let it go with the hope that it will fizzle out to a friendship thing.

Before they head out Hudson, sent me the recording. I need to talk to Bailey before she goes to the attorney. How do I tell this woman that everything she knew was a lie? Maybe she already knows.

I plug the name Regina Morris into some different search engines. She is married to Justin Morris, a real estate agent in Long Island. He's a million dollar producer, big whoop. She doesn't work, typical trophy wife. Her maiden name was Maximiliano. Her family came to the States from Colombia. She has a brother, Mateo, and when I dig a little bit further, I find out he is a programmer for a large computer company. That just made the hair on the back of my neck stand up. My conversation with Travis replays in my head. This just got a lot more interesting. I glance at the time; if I leave now, I can make it home for dinner with my family. That is the joy of working only a few blocks from home.

When I get home, I find MJ and Andy in a heated discussion. Siblings know just what hot buttons to push. Stella has Patrick in his carriage and is wheeling him around the house. She has on MJ's heels and let's not even discuss her make-up. In her mind, Patrick is a living doll that she can take care of like her own. I grab a beer and join in playing with the kids. I learned a long time ago when MJ and Andy are going at it, it's best if I take a step back.

"Stella, what are we playing?" She has gotten so good at reading lips I don't have to slow it down at all.

"We are playing house. I'm the mommy and Patrick is the baby."

I take a seat at the little table she has set up next to her pink kitchen. I thank God they never had this stuff when we were kids, otherwise, MJ would've had Andy and I playing house with her every day.

"So, who am I today?" Yesterday I was the mailman, so it's always safe to ask.

"Today you are Father O'Neil. Now it's time for coffee. You can sit next to Sam."

Patrick has fallen asleep and I take a seat next to Sam the bear. Stella gives me a mini cupcake, except something's missing.

"Stella, what happened to all the frosting?"

"I had to taste it to make sure it wasn't poison. That's what daddy does to mine all the time. Uncle Fitz, who would put poison in frosting?" She throws her hands up in the air and I'm biting my lip, trying not to laugh. When I look up, Andy and MJ are in the doorway, laughing.

"Well, it's so nice that the two of you want to join us. Patrick gave up and fell asleep."

They each take a seat at the tiny table. These are the moments that make me feel alive. It's not stuff; it's having something money can't buy: love and kindness. That's what makes me a wealthy man.

MJ's talking snaps me out of my *ahh* moment.

"Hello, Fitz, are you with us? What happened with Gail?"

"I'm looking into something for a friend of hers. Besides that, she threw a dart at a map and is leaving in a couple of days for Paris—alone. What were you two arguing about?"

"Dogs."

"That's it, dogs?"

"I want to get Stella a dog, and your wife thinks I'm nuts." When MJ and Andy disagree, MJ's my wife and not his sister.

"Why don't you tell him the whole story. He wants to get her a pit bull. And before you jump all over me, my objection has nothing to do with the breed. I know that the dog is a reflection of the owner. I just think she should get a little dog. One that she can play house with."

"Fitz, you and I both know that she just wants a small dog to dress up cuz Dad never let you have a dog."

"Why don't you take Stella to one of the rescue shelters to see which dog she wants. It's her companion; she should have the final say in it," I suggest. MJ leans over and kisses me. Stella giggles. I snag the last cupcake with frosting off of Andy's plate, which makes Stella laugh even harder.

"That sounds like a great idea. Now, why are your balls in a twist over Gail going to Paris alone? She's an adult and she doesn't take foolish chances." Typical Andy—direct and to the point.

"Look, Andy, I don't know what my problem is. Maybe it's this case she has me looking into. I'm just off about everything today."

"What's the case?"

"I'm not sure, yet. It's a puzzle that I need to figure out. So far, everything I've found out is not going to be good for her friend. Let me ask you something; why do you think people cheat?"

"Well, that's out of left field. Apparently, your case has to do with someone cheating."

"It didn't start out that way. Once I started digging, I uncovered some stuff that I know will hurt their entire family and destroy some friendships. I just think that when you go into a marriage it has to be one hundred percent for life. It's easier to walk away then it is to stay. Yeah, sometimes there is a legit reason to get out, but . . ."

MJ gets up and signs to Stella to come with her. "Stella and I are going to get dinner ready. You guys can have some private time to talk."

I watch them leave as I pop my cupcake in my mouth. The frosting really is the best part.

"Let me ask you this, is there anyway you can work this case without telling your client about the cheating?"

"You know me; I don't lie. Besides, if your husband had another family that you didn't know about, would you want to know about it or go through life like an ostrich with your head in the sand?"

"You know that's not true right? They wouldn't be able to breathe. They dig a whole and put their eggs in it. They put their heads in the hole to turn them."

"When the hell did you become an ostrich whisperer?"

"Stella and I watch the *Discovery Channel* and *National Geographic* a lot."

"Back to my dilemma; would you want to know?"

"Are there children involved?"

"Yes, on both sides. Apparently, they are friends, but I don't know how much everyone knows."

"Man, that's some fucked up shit. I would want to know. Now, tell me what is really bugging you about Gail's trip?"

"I wish I knew. I just have that bad feeling I get sometimes, and you know that's never good. I tried to talk her out of it but she has her mind set on going."

Patrick begins to wake up, his blue eyes sparkling. "Little man needs a diaper change."

"You're on your own." Andy laughs and hightails it out of the room.

"Guess it's just us."

I love spending time with my kid, but the whole diaper thing is another story. I take him out of the stroller to assess the situation. At least this time it's not a bad one. We're only at DEFCON five. I make sure MJ ends up with the DEFCON one. I've got this diaper change thing down pat; in just a few minutes, we are good as new.

I know I have to call Bailey before Monday, but I'm dreading it. "Oh, little man, always be honest. You'll get so much further in life if you are true to yourself and the person you're with." I pick him up and turn to leave. MJ is standing in the doorway. "How long have you been watching us?"

"Long enough. Do you want to talk to me about it?"

"Not really. I know what I have to do; I'm just dreading it. I'm going to call her and see if I can meet her tonight. I have to tell her before she goes to the attorney on Monday."

I pass her Patrick and take out my phone. "I'll only be a minute."

"Dinner will be ready in five."

She leaves as I call Bailey. "Hi, Bailey. I know we were going to meet Monday afternoon, but I have some information I need to go over with you before that."

"Can't you just tell me over the phone?"

"I'd rather not. I can come to your house tonight, if that's possible?"

"I'm going to Gail's house tonight to help her with some last minute packing. My kids won't be with me, so why don't you meet me there."

I would suggest something private but knowing the news I'm delivering, it might be better to have Gail with her for support. "What time?"

"Is nine good?"

"Yes, I'll see you then."

I head into the kitchen and find Andy took over the cooking while MJ and Stella are looking at dogs on her tablet. I venture to say it's only a matter of time before MJ will try to convince me that we need a dog, too.

"Fitz, are you okay?"

I realize Andy's been talking to me. "Sorry, lost in thought."

"I asked if you were staying home long enough to eat with us."

"Yeah, I don't have to be at Gail's until nine." I try to have dinner with my family every night. These are the things that they will remember. Making everyday memories that will last a lifetime.

CHAPTER
SEVEN

Bailey

W HEN I PULL UP TO Gail's house, it lights up like a Hollywood premier. I could never live like this. My kids would be setting off the lights all hours of the day and night just to drive our neighbors crazy.

I'm curious about Fitz. Gail never mentioned him, but when she talked about missing her chance with him, her eyes were filled with such sadness. To think she's been friends with him for all these years and was never able to tell him how she really feels.

The garage opens and Gail motions me to pull in.

"Hey, you're early."

"Yeah, Fitz called me and wants to meet with me before I go to the attorney on Monday. I told him to come here since my kids were staying home. I brought pizza and wine." Just the mention of his name and her whole demeanor changes. Now I'm even more curious about him.

"Wow, maybe he already solved the puzzle, Bailey. That would be fantastic!"

"I hope so. Hell, maybe I'll get some money out of all of this." I pass her the pizza and grab the wine from the back before following her inside. Her home is open concept, always warm and inviting. Tonight, she has the fireplace going. We dig into the food and after polishing off half the pizza and the entire bottle of wine, I'm finally feeling relaxed.

"So, tell me why you decided on Paris?"

"I threw a dart and that's where it landed. Besides, Paris is the city of lights. I heard Christmas there is really something to see. Have you ever been there?"

My eyes grow large at the thought of someone just throwing a dart and going where it landed. "Yes, I did a lot of traveling when I was modeling. Some places were great and others a *nightmare*. But, Gail, the dart thing freaks me out!"

"Why?"

"What if it landed in the middle of the Sahara Desert?"

She throws her head back and laughs. "Bailey, you know me, I'm not that brazen. I would have thrown it again."

The bell rings, but not before the entire yard lights up. I don't think I could ever get used to that. Gail goes to answer the door while I open another bottle of wine. I turn around. Standing in the doorway is a man who doesn't look like *anything* I expected. I was thinking he might be geeky, kind of like Sheldon from the *Big Bang Theory*. He's anything but geeky, as he fills the entire doorway. Gail introduces us. I shake off my thoughts and offer him some wine, which he politely declines. We head into the living room and get comfortable by the fire.

"So, tell me, Fitz, have you figured out what was on that paper?"

"I'll give you some privacy," Gail states as she gets up but I take her arm and gently pull her back down.

"I want my friend with me. Especially if it's bad, which based on the grim look on Fitz's face, it must be really bad."

He gets up and heads to the fridge, grabs a bottle of water before coming back to his seat. "I can tell you that it appears to be part of a key. Keys don't need to be physical keys that we put into a lock. They can also be a string of code that when put together, opens something. What you found is only part of it. We need to find the rest of it to find out what it opens. Did you look through his office stuff again after you found it? Did you find anything else that, thinking about it now, would make you question it?"

He's peppering me with questions like a drill sergeant. Not what I was expecting but, then again, I really didn't know what to expect.

"I didn't look through the office boxes yet. It all seemed like basic office stuff, along with all his case files."

He glances at Gail and then back to me. This must be when he tells me the bad stuff. "How much do you know about Regina Morris and her husband?"

"She is married to Justin. Her daughter Megan and my daughter Lilly are best friends; they are in the same class. Justin sells high dollar real estate and Regina is a stay-at-home mom. Why? What does any of this have to do with them?"

His eyes are fixed on mine the entire time. He's not giving anything away. But I feel a chill run up my spine. He glances between Gail and me again.

"Look I'm a big girl, just tell me what you've found out. I can't imagine what could be so bad. I mean, Emerson went to work and came home every day."

He takes a deep breath and slowly exhales. "Apparently, Emerson and Regina hooked up. He ended it right away, but then she showed up pregnant. She claimed Megan is Emerson's daughter. Your husband set up two different trusts. One for you and your children and one for Megan. I'm sure when you go to the lawyer on Monday, you will find this all out. If he doesn't volunteer the information, you need to press him on it. Now, that I know your husband was hiding all of this in plain sight; I really need to go through the stuff from his office."

My head begins to spin. I'm not sure if it's from the wine or the fact that my husband was unfaithful to me with my—friend. All of their names are swirling around inside my head. I get up, race to the bathroom, drop to my knees, clutch my stomach and proceed to kiss the porcelain god. How could he? Why would he? With my friend!

I think I'm finally done. I've got nothing left in me, but now it hits me—the thought of how this is going to affect my children—Lilly. I clutch my stomach again and now the dry heaves take over.

"Why, Emerson, why? What did she give you that I couldn't?" When the hell did he find the time to do it? I smack my forehead as if that would force the stupidity out of my brain. Bailey, you ass, if a person really wants to cheat, they will find a way.

After a while there is a light tap on the door. "Bailey, I know this is a stupid question, but are you okay?"

"Okay? Am I okay? Gail, I've been duped, living in a world of lies. I don't know if I'll ever be okay." Well, that was probably more than she was bargaining for.

"Take as much time as you need. There is a spare toothbrush in the vanity, along with some other toiletries. "

I get up and begin to freshen up. I still don't know what else my husband was into. The last thing I need right now is a pity party. I have three children that are depending on me to keep my shit together. *"Bailey, put your big girl panties on and face the music."* I take a deep breath, exhaling it before I head back into the living room.

"I'm sorry that I ran out on you, Fitz. What else have you found out?" I quickly take a seat next to Gail. Like she could be some sort of barrier to protect me from any more bad news.

"Nothing really, I just didn't want you to go into your meeting with the lawyer and get sucker punched."

"Do you think it's true?"

"Right now, I have no reason to doubt it. However, I want to dig further into this. If I am to believe that he accepted Regina's claim and didn't question it, I want to know why."

"Do you think she was blackmailing him? He left me in so much debt, I can't imagine she could get anything from him."

"Until I can look into everything, all I could do is guess and that's not something I subscribe to. He set up the two trusts, so he might not be as broke as you think. Until I can figure this all out, do not let her know that you know any of this. I need to get going, I'll meet you at your house Monday after your visit with the attorney."

He gets up to leave, and Gail walks him to the door. I finally snap out of my pity fog (for lack of better words) and run after him. He's about to get on his bike. I shout out to him, "Fitz, wait!" He stops, turns around and our eyes meet. I don't want him to see how scared and desperate I am. I quickly look down. "Um, can you possibly go with me? I mean, I'll pay you for your time." My voice cracks. I'm sure he now knows I'm scared. He heads toward me and puts both his hands on my shoulders.

"That won't be necessary, if you're sure you want me there."

"Yes!" I squeak out, interrupting him.

Gail puts her arm around my waist; the support is reassuring. "My flight for Paris is not until Tuesday evening. I'll go with you, too. Fitz, I'll meet you at Bailey's house and we can go in my car. Trust me, Bailey, you'll thank me later."

He begins to laugh and heads back to his bike.

"Eventually, Gail, I'm going to get you on Wanda. It's just a matter of time."

And with that, he's gone, like the whirlwind he came in on.

CHAPTER
EIGHT

FITZ

I HATED TO DUMP EVERYTHING on Bailey, but she needs to know the truth. Gail can be trusted, so I'm glad she is there for her. Although, come Tuesday, she'll be on her way to Paris.

Traffic is light tonight. I put on the new playlist MJ made me. David Garrett playing "Stairway to Heaven" booms loudly. I never thought I would like instrumental music, but when I'm working a case, I can focus without the words getting in the way.

Why would Emerson just agree the kid is his? Especially in to-day's world when a paternity test is no big deal. Bailey seemed genuinely surprised about the kid and the affair. I wonder how close Bailey is to Regina? How does Regina's husband, Justin, play into all of this? Rule of thumb is to follow the money. Question is, where did Emerson get the large amounts of cash? Ruby said whenever she told him they needed money, he would come through the next day with large sums. Drugs? Maybe, maybe not. How much does

Regina know? What could this code possibly do? *Regina is the key.*

I pull up to the house. As I head up the steps to the front door, the lights come on. Thankfully, my neighbors are used to it, even the local, Mrs. Kravitz, feels safer that I'm here. When I finally get inside, I find MJ asleep on the couch. Andy is long gone. I pick up the baby monitor and look at the video of my son; Patrick is fast asleep. A bomb could go off and that kid will sleep right through it. I scoop MJ up, and her arms instantly go around my neck as she pulls me in for a kiss. Words could never describe what she is to me. All I know is she makes me whole. I carry her to our bedroom as she nuzzles into my neck.

"I tried to wait up for you."

"I'm sorry. I didn't think I would be this late." I put her on the bed and pull off her t-shirt. I make quick work of my own clothes, tossing them on the floor next to hers.

"I know how hard it is for you to deliver bad news. How did your client take it?"

"Bailey took it about as bad as I expected. This was just the tip of the iceberg. She's been betrayed in the worst possible way. I'm sure it will be very difficult to come back from this, especially when the reality of it all finally sinks in." We snuggle under the covers and I hold her tightly. More so then usual.

"That bad?"

"Her husband had an affair with her friend. The friend got pregnant and now the kids are best friends, only they have no idea they are siblings."

"That's really fucked up. How did Gail handle it?"

"Alright, I guess. It wasn't her husband," I answer as she runs her fingers up and down my chest.

She stops and looks up at me with a look that makes me question if I'm a total moron. "Sometimes you're so dense. These women are her friends. Friends don't do this; it rocks the entire dynamics of the group. Gail doesn't have family or a significant other. These friends are her family. Now things have been disrupted."

"Well, hell, I never thought of it like that. The only friend I had growing up was Andy and he bats for the other team, so I never had anything to worry about. Besides, I've only ever loved you."

"Like I said—dense. What about Bailey?"

I pull her in closer to me. "What about her?"

"Well, I know if it were me, I would make sure the children didn't pay the price for their father's mistake."

"That's because you are a tender-hearted person."

"I would find you on your way to the pearly gates and kick your ass."

I throw my head back and laugh, because I know she would find a way to do just that. "I love how you love me so fiercely." I wrap her around my body and kiss her deeply. She hums, sending vibrations straight to my cock.

I've heard talk at the station that when you're married for a while, you fall into a routine. Especially when there are kids involved. However, with MJ, it's always explosive. I don't think it will ever change for us.

She's on top of me. I'm mindlessly stroking her back. I'm content in every way that counts. I'm living my dream. How many people can say that? She works her way down my chest, taking one of my nipples between her teeth. She tugs at it, not hard but just enough for the other one to get jealous. She continues kissing me everywhere but then stops at my tattoo. It used to be a simple *Superman* emblem that I got as a teenager just for her. However, thanks to Mark Chambers, a bat-shit-crazy serial killer, it now has, what looks like, a streak of fire running through it.

"You'll always be my hero," She whispers before nipping at it, leaving a trail of kisses from one hip to the other. She gently takes a hold of my cock, her tender lips kissing the tip followed up with the swirl of her tongue. Her mouth is warm and her touch is soft. The slower she goes, the harder my cock gets. She slides my cock to the back of her throat—throat bump. If there is one thing that will literally drive me insane, it's the throat bump. She knows what it does to me and yet, she teases me with it.

"Babe, if you keep doing that, I'm going to come so hard, my balls are going to shoot out the tip of my dick. After that, I can pretty much guarantee I'll be a one-shot-wonder tonight." She gives it one more slow slide along her tongue before she climbs on top of me and guides me into her coochie.

"You're in control, MJ, do whatever you want," I announce. She's smiling like a Cheshire cat. It's surreal watching her in control, doing whatever she wants to pleasure us both.

Totally sheathed deep inside of her, she stops, rakes her nails up and down my abs. Now she begins to rock back and forth. She's working herself into a frenzy. Finally, she leans back giving me full access to her. I work the pad of my thumb round and round her clit. This makes her moan and it causes a chain reaction right down to the root of my cock.

"Oh, MJ, up and down babe, slow and easy." Every time she goes up, I pull her down hard as I push my hips up to meet her.

"Oh, God, Fitz, harder, baby, I won't break!" Her nails dig into my legs and she begins to shake. "Fitz! Yes, Fuck, yes!" She comes with such force that her whole body quivers. I find my release right behind her. She collapses on my chest, her wild, red mane sprawled all over it. Still buried deep inside her, she milks me for all she can get. The music is softly playing in the background but all I can hear is my heart pounding in my chest. There's a sheen of sweat on both of us. I know we need a shower, but we both can't move. After a while, I tilt her head up towards mine, and her face is flushed. I swear her freckles are brighter. I lean in, gently pressing my lips to hers. She deepens the kiss, and I feel my cock start to come back to life. I tilt my hips and she releases my lips while letting out a long, low throaty moan. Jesus, what she does to me is unreal.

"Fitz, I'll always want us to be just like this . . . so intense."

I roll us over so I'm on the top. "Now, I'm setting the pace. Nice and slow for me, babe." I begin to move and I realize the music playing softly in the background is one of my all time favorite songs, "Perfect," by Ed Sheeran, with Andrea Bocelli. She is perfect in every way and all mine. I feel my heart begin to race; I know I won't be able to hold back much longer. The moment is surreal. MJ arches her back, offering me her breasts like they are being served to me on a silver platter. I graze on one nipple and then the other.

"Fitz, I can't hold back."

My name on her lips is the only benediction I need as we both loose ourselves. I pull the covers over us and gently kiss her. "Sleep, my angel," I whisper as we both drift off.

CHAPTER
NINE

Bailey

IT'S SUNDAY MORNING, AND I can hardly lift my head off the pillow. I was hoping to wake up this morning to everything being a bad dream. No such luck. How could I ever tell my kids what's going on? How can I ever look at Regina and not want to kill her? And Lilly? My God, what do I tell her? *Your dad was not the perfect father you believed him to be. Oh, and your best friend Megan is really your half sister. That should go over big.*

Holy hell, do the others know? My stomach knots up. I feel the bile rise in my throat. I jump up and race to the toilet. There is nothing left inside of me; now for the dry heaves. There is a tap on the door followed by Ella stepping into the room, carrying a tray. God, I hope there's no food on it. I don't want to explain why I can't keep anything down. She puts the tray on the bed and waits for me to clean up a bit.

"Thanks, El. What did you bring me?" I stay at the sink, still trying to brush my teeth.

"Stuff for a hangover."

I stop brushing long enough to let what she said sink in. "I'm not hung over. I must have eaten something that didn't agree with me; it happens. How do you know so much about hangovers?"

She rolls her eyes as if I just asked the stupidest question of all time. "Google and Pinterest. You can find anything you want."

I give up on the brushing, crawl back into bed and pull the covers up. "Are you going to be home today?" I put on my best sad face and hope she feels sorry for me.

"Yeah, do you need something else?"

"I need to get some rest. Can you keep an eye on your brother and sister?"

"Sure." She heads out, already on her phone.

I could call Ruby and find out exactly what she knows, but I can't blame her for Emerson's indiscretion. If she was really worth her salt, she would have told me. I guess her loyalty always lied with Emerson and now it died with him.

All night long, Fitz's words kept swirling around in my head . . . *with your friend, Regina.* As much as I want to stay in bed, indefinitely, I need to get up and continue on with my life. My kids need me to keep it together. After all, I'm all they've got. I take a few sips from this God-awful Bloody Mary that Ella made. I have an idea: maybe I should go through Emerson's office stuff before Fitz comes tomorrow. There could be another clue hidden in plain site. It's not going to get done sitting in bed, having a pity party. I drag my ass into the shower, determined I'm not going to let him destroy my life anymore then he already has.

After standing in a hot shower until the water ran cold, I'm finally ready to face the kids. I head downstairs and the only one there is Ella.

"Hey, where is everyone?"

"Collin had practice and Lilly is at Megan's house."

That's the last place I want her to be, but for now I need to keep my mouth shut and my feelings to myself.

"What are you up to?"

"I'm leaving in a few minutes to meet some girls from my study group."

"Okay, but make sure you're back before dark."

She gives me the teenage eye roll again and a quick wave as she heads out the door. I trust her. She's never given me cause to doubt her. But the same can be said for Emerson and look where that got me. I get up to chase after her but stop myself when I get to the door. *Bailey, don't dump your insecurities on Ella.* Geez, now I'm talking to myself. I head down the hall to the office with Sad Sack following closely behind me. I take a deep breath before I step inside. I don't know what I'm afraid of. I've already gone through the personal stuff and Ro went through all the financial stuff. I take in a quick sharp breath of surprise. Oh. My. God. Does Ro know? I know Gail was just as shocked as I was. We are such a close group and I would like to think if one of us had this bombshell information, we would call the person out in front of all of us. Now Regina's odd behavior Friday night makes more sense. Maybe it wasn't too much to drink. Maybe it was too much guilt.

I spend the next three hours going through every piece of paper, along with every file on his computer—nothing. There is one thing I can't get into and that is his cloud. It's password protected. I try to put in something that I think Emerson would use but it's no good. I only get two more tries before I'm locked out. I close it down and put it aside for Fitz.

After meeting him, I can understand why Gail was so taken with him. His presence fills the room and his looks are strong, yet, endearing.

I'm sitting on the floor with stacks of papers around me and the picture of Emerson and me in my lap. We were so in love. Knowing what I know now, it makes me wonder what else in my life was a total lie? *"Emerson, how could you do this to us, to your family?"* I shout out through my tears. Like I'm expecting the dead to answer me. If only it was that easy. Sad Sack lifts his head, reaches in and licks my tears. He's the only male I know I can count on.

I glance at the clock. It's late and no one is home yet. It's starting to get dark. I hate the dark. Just as I reach for my phone, I hear the front door open and the kids' bickering fills the air. Normalcy . . . the only normal I know I can count on.

Monday morning rolls around and I get the kids off to school. The house is empty and quiet. It's times like these, I wish I had a sibling. Someone I could trust. I thought I could trust my friends but I see how well that turned out. I have time before everyone will be here. As I head downstairs, Sad Sack races in front of me. "Damn it, dog! You're lucky I didn't break my neck," I snap. He stops at the front door, sits down, and begins a low growl. Then I hear the bell ring, along with a knock on the door. I look out and see Regina. Shit, how the hell am I going to keep it together? Fitz said not to let her know. That is easier said than done. Maybe I'll pretend I'm not home.

"Bailey, I know you're in there. Open up, please."

I stay ramrod straight, holding my breath.

"Bailey, I just want to apologize for the other night. Open up!"

Sad Sack's growl gets louder. I don't need her making a scene for the neighbors. As I gather up all my strength, I slowly open the door.

"Sorry, I was in the back of the house." Fitz's words keep replaying in my mind.

"Are you going to invite me in?" she asks. I step aside and open the door wider for her. "I wanted to apologize for the other night. I had way too much to drink."

Looking at her, I can't figure out what the hell Emerson was thinking? I mean, not to toot my own horn, but I was a fashion model for some of the top designers in the world. She's ordinary. Maybe that's what he really wanted—ordinary.

"We all had too much to drink. Let's just put it behind us. I would offer you some coffee, but I have an appointment."

"Is it anything I can help you with?"

Bitch, I think you helped yourself to enough. I'm trying to figure out how to quickly get rid of her when I hear the roar of a motorcycle as Fitz pulls into the driveway. Regina steps just outside the front door. Her mouth is hanging open as Fitz takes off his helmet and gets off of his bike. In the light of day, I can honestly say he is all that and then some.

"Hey, Bailey, am I interrupting something?"

"No, Fitz, this is my friend, Regina. She's just getting ready to leave."

He steps closer and offers her his hand. She finally stops staring long enough to shake it.

"How do you know, Bailey?"

Nosey bitch. I'm finding it hard not to rip her apart. Fitz puts his arm around my shoulders and gives it a slight squeeze.

"Mutual friends. Bailey, you ready?"

I'm gathering that's his polite way of saying *take a hike, bitch.*

"Oh, okay, um do you want to get together for dinner?" She's stalling, no doubt wanting to know more about Fitz.

"Tonight is not good, but I'll call you later," I say before Fitz practically closes the door in her face.

"I trust you followed my instructions regarding her."

"Yes, it took all of me not to bitch slap her. I'll put up a pot of coffee while you get started going through Emerson's stuff. Just to let you know, I looked at everything last night and the only oddity I found was that I could not get into his cloud account. It's password protected." We head towards the office and Sad Sack is all over him like he has a new best friend. *Traitor.*

"Did you try opening it?"

"Of course I did. I tried once and I got the password wrong. It only gives three attempts to open it up before the account is locked. I didn't want to take anymore chances. "I'll leave you alone; let me know if you need anything." I open the office door and step aside. He heads in, looks around but doesn't seem to upset by the amount of file boxes everywhere.

"Good, I'll start with his computer."

I leave him to go through everything while I head to the kitchen.

CHAPTER
TEN

FITZ

I'M STANDING IN A VERY typical home office. Typical except for the fact that the owner is dead and took his secrets and lies to the grave with him. The man had a lot of paper files and they are stacked in boxes all around the room. No way I'm getting through all of this myself. Time to call in reinforcements.

Me: Hey, I need you to try and get into my client's husband's cloud account.

Travis: . . .

Me: He's dead and the wife has possession. She has agreed to let me try to get into it any way possible.

Travis: Good, I'd like to keep my day job. It's kind of scary when you can read my thoughts.

Me: What do you need from me?

Travis: Tell me about the computer.

Me: It's a MacBook pro.

Travis: Give me his email address and I can request access from you.

I quickly give him everything he needs, and now I'm watching him move around through the computer.

Travis: It's not a quick thing. This might take me a bit.

Me: Okay I'll leave it open but I've got to go with my client to her attorney's office. I'll check back with you later.

Travis: Okay, good luck.

I disconnect with him and take another look around the room. Why the hell did this man keep so much paper? I'll get Hudson to help me. She needs to learn the less than glamorous side of the business.

Me: Hey, I need your help again.

Hudson: Class is over at 1:00. Can it wait until then?

Me: Yeah, I need you to go through all of Emerson's paper files. Bailey has them stacked in boxes in his home office. I have to go to the lawyer with her. I'll text you the address.

Hudson: Sal is picking me up, so send him the address. What am I looking for?

Me: I'm not sure. Just check to see if anything looks off. You already know the situation. I'll let Bailey know what is going on.

Hudson: Okay, ttyl.

There is a tap on the door. It's Bailey, coffee in hand. "Thank you," I take the coffee, "I've got my friend working on getting into his cloud account. We need to make sure we leave the computer open. My associate is coming by this afternoon to go through the files."

"My kids will be here." Her desire to protect her kids no matter what is not lost on me.

"Would you rather they take the files back to the office?"

"No, I'll be here later and I'll explain it to them, somehow."

"We can tell them that the files are being audited before they are handed over to a new attorney," I suggest.

She takes a step back and her eyes narrow. Somehow, I feel like I've offended her. "That came easy for you. Do you always twist the truth?"

"Ouch, that stings. No, I'm probably the most honest and direct person you will ever meet. However, I'm also a parent. Being a parent has upped my game. I understand the need to protect them, no matter what." That seems to satisfy her. I need to steer the conversation on to something else. "Why don't you tell me about the different stacks of boxes you've got going here."

"There wasn't much money left in his bank accounts, so I had to close up the office rather quickly. Ruby helped me box everything up. I brought them here and after I went through them, I boxed them up the same way she packed them. Is that important?"

"Shouldn't be, I was just curious. Later, I'm going to take his computer with me. By the time we get back, my friend should be done with it.. You know the more I look around here, the more I think it would be better to take all of these boxes back to my office. I'll let my team know and you won't have to worry about explaining anything to your kids."

"If it helps you, then go for it."

The dog is on his back with his ass resting on my feet. He begins to wiggle and then lets out an odd noise. "It seems your dog likes me."

"Yeah, about that; Sad Sack is a traitor. He's not proud; he'll beg anyone for a belly rub."

"Sad Sack? Who names a dog Sad Sack?"

"We rescued him during a snow storm. He had such a sad look on his face. As a joke I called him that and it stuck."

The ringing doorbell makes him leap up and as he runs towards the door, he spins around trying to catch his tail. Gifted, for sure.

Gail steps in. "Sorry, I thought I would be able to get here earlier but I had a conference call that went over."

"Don't worry; we don't have too far to go." Bailey says as we make our way to the front door to follow Gail to her car. She gives Gail the address for her GPS and in no time, we are on our way.

"Bailey, how did you find this attorney?" I question her about everything and anything because sometimes the little things come to mean so much more later on.

"He went to law school with Emerson. He handled every thing for us. Is that important?"

"I'm just curious. You don't have to question everything in your life, that's my job."

"Well, apparently, I should have been doing that. Maybe then my husband would have been faithful to me."

Gail cringes at Baileys words but she keeps her eyes on the road and her mouth shut. We pull up to a small cottage-type house in town. Very nondescript and not what I was expecting. When we step inside, we're greeted by one of the Stepford wives. Well, not really one of the Stepford wives; that's the name I give to all girls on the north shore of Long Island—blonde, fake tan, and fake boobs. We are ushered in to Claude Stanford's office. Bailey and Gail take a seat while I nosey around the room. Claude finally comes into the room, flustered, probably for making us wait.

"I'm sorry, I was on a call and couldn't get away any sooner. I'm just back from vacation and it's nuts trying to catch up. Bailey, I was shocked to hear about Emerson. They said he had a heart attack, did he have heart problems in the past?"

"No, it was very sudden."

"Sad. So, you're here about his will and the trust. Would you like to do this in private?" He cocks his head and focuses on me, never asking who I am or if I would like a seat. Already, I don't like him.

"Gail and Fitz are here for my support. Anything you have to say can be said in front of them."

He shuffles some papers and then pulls out a file from the bottom of the pile. "Well, it's pretty straight forward. It is a standard will that leaves everything in the trust to Ella, Lilly, and Collin. You are the guardian of the trust. However, he put in a clause, stating that you can request a distribution of funds, but it must be approved by me first. In the event of my death, Jake Daniels will take over. The value of the trust, as of today, is five million. The IRAs and the insurance policy list you as the beneficiary. Everything else of material value goes to you, including the house in Brookville, and the beach house in St. John's."

Bailey begins to shake and Gail grabs her hand. Apparently, something Claude said threw her for a loop.

"We are here for you; we'll get through this."

"Do you need a minute or would you like me to continue?"

"Please, Claude, continue." She takes a few deep breaths and keeps her eyes focused on him.

"About three months ago, he gave me a letter to give to you in the event he passed before you." He pulls an envelope out of the file and passes it to Bailey. She takes it from him and puts it in her purse.

"Bailey, if there is anything I can do for you, please don't hesitate to ask." He looks at his watch and back to her. He's about to give her the blow off—*bastard*.

"I have another appointment waiting. My assistant, Heidi, will have papers for you to sign, and then you can get on with your life."

Get on with her life? What kind of fucking asshole is this moron? He gets up and heads towards the door. I'm about to step in and stop him from leaving but Bailey gets out of her chair so fast that it tumbles over.

"Get on with my life? You're not going anywhere until you explain some stuff to me. How about telling me about the other trust he has set up for his illegitimate child, Megan?"

His face turns pale and he tries to hide his surprise. Probably not about the trust but the fact that Bailey knew about Megan.

"Yeah, I know that he had a child with my friend behind my back! And while we are on the subject of secrets, a beach house?! Five million in a trust, where the fuck did he get that kind of money? How much is the trust for Megan worth? What the hell else was he hiding? What was he really into? Does Jake know about all of this?" She's yelling and shaking. This was her time to get answers and instead all she got were more questions. Gail is trying to calm her down but right now, Bailey is finding it hard to breathe.

"Bailey, please calm down. I swear I only know what he chose to share with me. I know the mistake he made with Regina ate away at him. He never wanted the children to suffer because of him. I think that's why he signed over his parental rights to Regina's husband Justin. As far as how he made his money, I just assumed he was a damn good lawyer. I don't know how much Jake knows."

I step towards the door and my size virtually blocks the whole doorway. "Answer her questions—*now!*"

"Look, all that information is confidential. The best thing you can do is sign the papers and, yes, get on with your life. Now, let me pass or I'll call the cops, and have you arrested."

Bailey gets up and pulls me towards her. "Fitz, let him go."

"Are you sure that's what you really want?"

"Yes. He was Emerson's friend, and at this point, I wouldn't be able to trust anything he tells me."

I step aside, letting him rush out the door. Heidi comes in with the papers she needs Bailey to sign. It's just a standard release.

When we get to the car, I open the door for her but stop her from getting in. "I'm going to need to know what is in that letter he left you. I'm sure it's personal, but there could be some sort of clue as to where he got the money from."

She nods and quickly gets into the car. Thankfully, Gail drove and the ride back to Bailey's house is deathly silent. This is the part of my job that I hate. When my clients fall apart because of someone else's actions.

When we get back to Bailey's house, Sal and Hudson are waiting. I make the introductions and then everyone heads inside, but I hold Sal back. I quickly fill him in on everything.

"Okay, I'll comb through the files with Hudson. You said there is a lot of them, so I'm sure we'll be at it for a while."

Each of the partners at the agency has a specialty. Sal is the computer wizard. Travis, although not a partner, does a lot of work for the agency when he's not tied up with his day job at the FBI. Between the two of them, nothing will stay buried. We head inside and help load all the boxes into the car. I'm glad we were able to get it all done before Bailey's kids got home.

"When I'm done here, I'll meet you back at the office," I say before they leave.

I head inside to find out what was in the letter. Instead, I find Bailey has fallen apart and Gail is trying her best to console her, but she doesn't seem to be making any headway.

"Bailey, we were able to get all the boxes out of here before your kids get home. But none of that is going to matter if you don't pull yourself together. Now, what was in the letter?"

"I need a drink." She gets up, takes the letter and slaps it to my chest.

Gail follows her to the bar she has set up in her family room. She pours her a rather large glass of brandy. I look at the letter; it's only one page.

Bailey,

If you're reading this letter, then unfortunately, I'm dead. I have to confess something to you, Bailey. I had a one-time indiscretion with Regina. You have to believe me, sweetheart, it was only one time, but

I guess once was enough. I don't even remember it happening. I was weak and I fear my weakness may have put our family in jeopardy.

She called me and asked to meet with me to discuss a divorce. She didn't want to come to the office. She was afraid she would be seen. We met for dinner at a small place she picked. She wanted to divorce Justin because he is sterile. She said not being able to have a child was a game changer for her. I tried to counsel her to stay with Justin and try to work things out. I wanted her see she still had a lot of options, but she wanted out. Honestly, I don't remember what happened after that. All I know is, I woke up and I was in a hotel bed with her. I tried to block it out of my head. I told her I couldn't represent her. I gave her a list of attorneys that would be able to do so. I thought that was it, but a couple of months went by and I couldn't live with myself. Every time I looked at you, I felt the guilt takeover. I called her and told her I was going to tell you everything. That same day, she showed up at my office, told me she was pregnant, and the baby was mine. I told her I wanted a paternity test and she handed me Justin's medical reports, showing he was indeed sterile. You were pregnant with Lilly. I didn't want to upset you. She said all she ever wanted was a child of her own. I decided to let Justin claim Megan as his own child. I thought it would be best for everyone involved.

In the beginning, I really believed she did it because she wanted to have a baby. I soon realized that couldn't be further from the truth. After Regina had Megan, she dangled her paternity in front of me like a carrot on a string. That's when the blackmail started. Regina and her brother Mateo got me mixed up in some illegal stuff. I'm not sure what Justin knows and, personally, I didn't trust him, either, so asking him was a waste of time. I knew I had to do something to guarantee my safety as well as yours and the kids. I thought if I kept you in the dark, it would keep you out of harms way.

So, I took other steps to keep everyone safe the only way I knew how. I documented everything I did for them. I included detailed ledgers and hundreds of questionable videos of some of the wealthiest and most influential people in the world. When I figured out Mateo's side business, I included that in the ledgers, too. I locked up everything someplace special that I knew they would never find. When Mateo found out about everything I had accumulated, he flipped out. He knew what I had was the Holy Grail of blackmail material. He was determined to find it, no matter what he and Regina had to resort to. Mateo is a dangerous man.

Finally, the reason I purchased the beach house. I told Jake I had the case that would make him a household name. He's my best friend and I knew I could trust him. I gave him a sample of the information I had, and he offered me a deal. I told him I just needed a little bit more time to get my house of cards in order. Jake agreed, and when everything was done, I could move us all to St. John's to start over. I planned on begging you every day for your forgiveness. But, I guess I never got the chance.

I really did love only you, Bailey. Please be careful and remember, not everyone is your friend. Trust your gut and keep the kids safe.

Love, Emerson

What the fuck did this guy get himself into? I've seen a lot of crazy shit, but this is just off the charts. It's like something out of a spy novel. Bailey seems to be a lot calmer. No doubt the brandy has finally kicked in. I snap a picture of the letter before I give it back to her. "Bailey, here's the letter. You might want to put it away before your kids get home."

"Maybe I should just burn it and forget all of this. Nothing is going to bring Emerson back to me. This fucked up mess will not change. In the end, Megan is still his daughter and she and Lilly are still best friends."

"I get your point, but please don't burn it. If you want, I'll take it with me."

She stares at it for a few seconds and then passes it back to me.

"Keep it along with all the other stuff. Like I said, nothing is going to change."

I take the letter and shove it into my pocket just as Sad Sack takes off running towards the door.

"He always knows when my kids will be walking through the door."

"I'm going to leave. I will contact you as soon as I know anything. Remember, Bailey, say nothing to Regina. Gail, have a safe trip and please check in along the way," I nag her one last time. She rolls her eyes as I pull her in for a hug. "Just humor me," I grumble under my breath.

"I head out the door and hop on Wanda. As I start to pull away from the house, I see the kids getting out of Regina's car. She is sitting behind the wheel, watching me like a hawk. I know Bailey wants to forget everything and move on, but unfortunately, that's not possible. Not until we know the truth, no matter how much it hurts.

CHAPTER
ELEVEN

Bailey

WITHIN MINUTES OF FITZ LEAVING, the kids come in, along with Regina and Megan. This is the hard part, keeping the secret from the kids. Gail jumps up, I grab her hand and squeeze. "Not now," I whisper so only she can hear.

The kids are laughing and enjoying snacks as Sad Sack, once again, believes he can catch his tail. Not saying anything to Regina is hard. I've never wanted to punch someone in the face until now. She comes into the family room and takes a seat across from Gail.

"So, was that cute guy on the motorcycle the guy I met earlier? I think you said his name is Fitz. Are you dating already, Bailey? You can tell me the truth."

I'm trying so hard to keep it together. I glance into the kitchen to see if my kids are listening, but they are busy on their phones. The last thing I need is for them to hear this conversation. I take a deep breath trying to calm myself, but before I can answer Gail puts her hand on my knee and gives it a gentle squeeze.

"Actually, Regina, he is a good friend of mine. I asked him to install an alarm system for Bailey like he did at my house. I felt, since she is alone now, she should have it." Gail is quick on her feet. But she's never been a good liar. Regina cocks her head as if she is contemplating her answer.

"So, you are going to stay in this house? I thought for sure you would want a new, more affordable place." She raises her voice when she stresses the word affordable. My blood pressure is rising by the second.

"I haven't decided what I'm going to do yet. For Christ's sake, Regina, he's only dead three months, and I would appreciate it if you didn't speak about my dating or my financial situation in front of my children. They have enough to deal with right now. They don't need your gossip."

The tension is so thick you can cut it with a knife.

"Calm down, Bailey, I'm not gossiping; I'm just trying to be supportive. Besides, the only thing the kids are paying attention to are their phones. I better get going. Gail, when do you leave for Paris?"

"Tomorrow, I'll walk you out. Bailey, I'll call you later."

I give her a hug and whisper, "Thank you." I close the door and when I turn around, Ella is in my face.

"You're dating?"

"I didn't think you heard that. No, I'm not dating anyone. Regina was looking for something to gossip about. I had a friend of Gail's here today. He is helping me with all of the stuff your father left behind. I'm not dating; I'm trying to get through the day. I promise you, dating is not even on my realm right now."

She's not moving, her eyes searching mine, no doubt looking for the truth. After a beat, she finally backs up and heads toward the kitchen. I think my answer satisfied her. At least, I hope it did.

I know I need to figure out this puzzle, but for tonight, I want to block it out of my head. I opt to grab a bottle of wine and head upstairs to soak in the tub.

Regina

As we walk toward my car, Gail grabs my arm, stops, and twists me around to face her.

"Megan, get in the car, I'll be there in a minute." We both watch her get in the car and before I can say anything, Gail's grip gets tighter.

"Regina, Bailey has been through so much. I know you think you're helping, but you're not. She needs our support. We're the only family she has left. Why the hell would you say that about dating in front of the kids? On top of that, she's trying to keep the roof over their heads and you are tossing around the idea that she should sell her home. It's the only home those kids have ever known. You need to keep your mouth shut and maybe put those kids before your need to gossip!"

"Oh, for Christ's sake, I'm not gossiping. Maybe everyone should stop tiptoeing around her and be realistic. The bottom line is: she can't afford to maintain that house. She has no skills to go back into the workforce. Her looks are still holding up, maybe she can use that to find another man to latch on to. Face the facts, Gail; sitting on the sidelines won't do her any good. Look where it got you."

Her hand came around so fast that I never saw it coming. I'm sure her handprint is now on my face—*bitch*.

"The truth hurts, Gail. Deal with it." I turn away, get in my car and take off, leaving her in the driveway. I'm tired of playing nice with everyone. I worked my way up from the streets of Bogota to what I have today. Why the hell does she think she's better than me? Is it because she has some fancy title? At the end of the day, she's alone and I'm not.

When I get home, I find Mateo parked outside, waiting for me. I pull into the garage. Megan gets out and runs into the house, paying no attention to me. I head toward his car and climb in for a chat. It's the best place to talk without anyone eavesdropping.

"What the hell took you so long? I've been here for an hour. What did you find out? Why is your face red?"

"Hello to you, too. I found out that she went to the attorney today. There is a guy that's been hanging around. When I asked about him, Gail said he's her friend and he's installing an alarm system."

"Do you believe her?"

"No, Gail can't lie to save her life. She only gave me his first name: Fitz. My face is red because Gail smacked me—hard. There is too much at stake, Mateo, we need to find out where Emerson hid everything, and it has to be soon."

"Why did she hit you? Did you deck her?"

"I called her out on her high and mighty bullshit and I guess the truth hurt."

"Maybe we can get some information from Gail."

He's not always the brightest bulb in the box.

"Did you hear a word I said? I really pissed her off and I doubt she'll talk to me and yet you think we can get some information from her. Don't you get it, she's actually lying for Bailey. That goes against everything miss goody-two-shoes stands for."

"I still think I might be able to get something out of her."

"Well, she leaves for Paris tomorrow. If you're going to do anything, it better be quickly."

"Give me her address and I'll handle her. I had one of my friends sit on Bailey's house today. A couple showed up and loaded up the car with file boxes. I venture to say they came from Emerson's office."

"Did he follow them?"

"No, his orders were to sit and watch. He did take photos and he got the plate number. I'll run it and figure out who they are. I don't think Emerson was stupid enough to keep it in his office but, then again, who knows? For now, try to get back in Bailey's good graces. While you're at it, try and get your hands on Emerson's computer, if it's even still there. I'll have my men track down those boxes."

"Oh yeah, that will go over big. Think, Mateo, why would she let me have his computer? Right now, she wants nothing to do with me."

"See, this is why I told you when you found out how much stuff he accumulated we should have taken it from him right then and there. Or, at least, we should have stored everything in a place where all three of us had access to it. Maybe you can use Megan, you've done it before with Emerson. Do the same thing with Bailey."

"If you remember correctly, we all agreed when we started that he should keep the financial ledgers because he was good at creative accounting. I only found out about the second set of ledgers, your side business, and the videos right before he died. I have no idea how he managed to get them on every one of our clients. If any of this was made public, lives would be ruined and our heads would be the first on the chopping block, literally. Did you find out how the hell he found out about your side business? You were supposed to be the only one handling it."

"I have no idea. He was a lot smarter than I thought. I'm more worried right now about the money. If we don't make a transfer soon, it will send up a red flag. If that happens, we're dead."

The last thing I want to think about is what his China connection will do to us if they're exposed.

"Look, I've got to get inside. See what you can find out from Gail. I'll talk to you tonight." I get out and quickly head inside the garage and close the door.

There is a light dusting of snow with a prediction of more. If the weather gets worse, the schools will close tomorrow, leaving me to deal with Megan all day. Truth be told, she is closer to Justin than to me. I never felt a bond with her. I never wanted children, Justin did. The lies that I keep are swirling around my head. Thanks to my brother's computer skills, Emerson believed Megan was his daughter. It was a big spin of the wheel. Luckily, she looks like me or I could have never passed her off to Emerson as his. *"Shake it off, Regina."* I need to find Emerson's part of the key, along with everything else he hid. Without it, the money sits in limbo. We each have a digital key and when we put them together, it unlocks the funds. The ledgers were Emerson's idea. I never had to worry about him using them against us, since I always held Megan over his head. God forbid if his precious Bailey finds the ledger. She is such a goody-two-shoes, she would turn it over to the authorities and then this whole house of cards will come tumbling down around all of us.

My husband believes the money comes from a trust I had from my grandparents. What an ass. I hope he's busy, so I don't have to deal with him. Lately, it's becoming harder and harder to string him along. I don't think he suspects anything but avoiding him is the better option. When I open the door, he is standing there waiting. So much for avoiding him.

"What took you so long?"

"I was cleaning the trash out of my car. Jesus, Justin, put a clock up my ass."

"Did you talk to Bailey about putting her house on the market?"

"I mentioned it to her, but she thinks she's going to be able to stay in the house for a while." I roll my eyes as I push past him. He's quick to follow at my heels, grabs my arm and spins me around.

"How the hell does she plan on doing that?"

"I don't know, maybe he had some insurance. I suggested she

sell it. Now, let go of me." I jerk my arm out of his grip and leave him standing there as I head upstairs. Without Emerson's part of the key, we are all fucked. Hopefully, Mateo will get something out of Gail.

Mateo

It's fucking freezing and my ass is stuck in this car, sitting outside Gail's house. I've got no clue what's going on inside. What I do have is access to her cell phone. People don't realize that their cell phone numbers are becoming more valuable then their social security numbers. There is an app for everything, including hacking into someone's phone without them knowing it. Her phone proves to be a plethora of information. There is a folder marked *work* that is password protected. If I can gain access to her case files, they can be very valuable to the right person. First things first, I need to figure out who Fitz is. I bring up her favorites and *bam* first name on the list, Fitzgerald S. Rodriguez. Thank you, Gail, for being so damn predicable. I search her phone a little bit more and find an app for a journal. Like I said, there's an app for everything. I read through some of it and it's about as boring as she is. I pull up her pictures and most of them are of food. There are some of her with her friends but none of them with a man. Now exactly who are you, Fitz?

I plug his name into a program on my laptop for finding out everything and anything on anyone I want. It doesn't take long for the hits to come—shit—he's a retired cop. Digging a little bit further and I find he's partners in The Cooper Agency, a Brooklyn based company that specializes in security and investigations. This is just fucking wonderful.

Me: I found out who Fitz is. He's a retired cop. It gets worse. He's partners in an agency that specializes in security and private investigations.

Regina: Maybe you're just being paranoid, looking for something bad around every corner. Maybe he really is installing a security system.

Me: Do you want to take that chance?

Regina: No, maybe she found the ledgers or the key. Damn it, you need to find out more!

Me: If she found the key, she wouldn't know what it is, so she can hire whom ever she wants. Without our keys, she's got nothing.

Regina: And if she finds the ledgers and the videos?

Me: That's all on you. I warned you not to let him keep anything. You thought dangling Megan's paternity was all you needed.

Regina: I never expected him to drop dead!

Me: Well, yeah, now I've got to clean up this mess. I'll handle Gail and this Fitz character, you take care of Bailey. I'll let you know what I find out.

Regina: Okay.

Gail's flight is for tomorrow night. I need to make sure she doesn't get on it. It looks like she ordered a private town car to take her to the airport—*perfect*. I quickly cancel it and monitor her email. As soon as the conformation for the cancelation comes in, I quickly delete it. Thankfully, I have a town car at my disposal to pick her up with. Now, I have to wait.

CHAPTER
TWELVE

FITZ

I F I HAD ANY THOUGHTS about sleeping in, Patrick squashed them. I need to teach him to sleep later so I can have my way with MJ in the morning. I love morning sex. Hell, I love all sex with MJ. I don't think that's too much to ask for. For now, she's sleeping in and I'm making him a bottle. "Buddy, we need to work on your timing. How am I supposed to make you a brother or a sister if you keep getting up before the sun does?" All that gets me is a *"da-da"* and him pulling my nose.

I spent the better part of last night going through the files with Hudson and Sal. All we got was a big fat zero. Oh, don't get me wrong; Emerson was making a large fortune handling divorces for the who's who of Long Island. He was also spending like someone who won the lottery. Eventually, all that shit catches up and Sal thinks that's where Emerson was at when he died. We still have about a dozen more boxes to go through, so maybe we will get lucky.

Patrick is almost back to sleep. A clean diaper and a full belly is all he ever needs. Just as I go to put him down, my phone rings and his eyes open wide. Damn it, I was so close to having my way with MJ.

"Travis, this better be a call with some good news."

"I got into the file on the guys computer, but I can't figure out what the hell it is. It's all in some sort of code. A code I've never seen before. It's not long, maybe some sort of instructions."

"What the hell was this guy into that everything is coded?"

"Before you go there, I already checked. He's not with any of the three letter alphabet agencies."

"I wasn't going to go there." Yeah, I was, but I don't want to give him the satisfaction of always being right.

"I call bullshit. Anyway, I emailed you what I found. Maybe have Sal mess around with it. He's really good at figuring that kind of stuff out. He's got a thing for cryptography."

"Alright, thanks."

He hangs up. Patrick is now wide-awake. "You know what, how about we make mommy breakfast in bed? That should earn me some husband sex points."

I'm glad he doesn't understand what I'm talking about. I put him down and in no time, he has a dozen toys all around him. Hopefully, I can earn enough points to cash in later. I've got the music going and I'm singing as I'm working on the food. In the corner of my eye, I catch Patrick dancing. Thank God he takes after his mother in that department. I join him and when I swing around MJ is standing in the doorway. I reach out and pull her into my arms. "My Girl" by Dylan Scott is on. I sing to her as I dance her around the kitchen. "*I can honestly say that she saved me.*" Those lyrics, right there, so true. As I spin her around again, Patrick starts clapping just as the smoke detector goes off from the bacon. So much for my husband sex points.

"Fitz, thank you. What a wonderful way to wake up."

"Even with the smoke alarm?"

"Of course. You keep life interesting."

Not exactly what I was going for, but I'll take it. I'm waving the towel over the smoke detector like a crazy man. Just as the noise stops, the doorbell rings. I can't catch a frigging break. I look at the monitor; it's Hudson, Sal, and my mom. I buzz them in and within minutes, the house is filled with laughter. Sometimes, life gets in the way of living and this is one of those times.

"Pull up a chair, the bacon is trashed but everything else is hot and ready. Why are you guys here so early?"

"There are still a dozen boxes that we didn't even touch last night. I wasn't sure how quick you needed them gone through, so I thought I would get an early start. Plus, your mom wanted to stop here on her way to church."

Hudson takes such good care of my parents. She's always helping them with one thing or another. She fills her morning with everything they need before she heads to work or school. I never have to ask her, she just does. She says it's no big deal, but to me, it is. It's like she's been a part of our family forever when, in reality, it's been a little over a year.

"I'm hoping you find something in those files. Maybe afterwards, you can reach out to Ruby and see if she knows anything else. She seemed to be comfortable talking to you, so maybe she will open up more."

"Yeah, I kind of felt like she had more to say but was unsure how much she should tell us. Maybe if it's just me, she'll be more comfortable."

"Do you think I intimidated her? I thought I was being so nice to her." I give her a cheeky smile and try not to burst out laughing.

"Actually, I think you did. I think it's because your disgust for cheaters and liars is not something you hide well."

"Wow, I didn't realize it was that apparent."

"Well it is. I'm going to walk Annie to church I'll be back in a few." She grabs a cup of coffee before she heads out.

"Sal, I spoke to Travis earlier and he was able to get into Emerson's cloud account. He found a file. He got it opened and it's some sort of letter, possibly instructions. However, it was in some kind of code. Nothing that Travis has ever seen. He said you have a thing for cryptography. I'll email it to you and maybe you can figure it out."

"Okay, while Hudson goes through the files, I'll mess around with it. In the meantime, what are we having for breakfast?"

I don't have a chance to answer. Andy comes in with Stella and now its mass chaos, but in a good way.

Gail

I'm a little nervous. Oh hell, who am I kidding? I'm very nervous. This is the first time I'm leaving the country. Fitz's apprehension about me going alone has pricked at my own doubts. I have let life's circumstances and my career guide me for too long. I know Fitz is living his dream and I'm truly happy for him. That ship for me sailed a long time ago. I procrastinated for so long about telling him how I felt. When I finally found the courage, it was too late. I know pining away for him for so long left me with blinders on for anyone else. Who knows what opportunities I've missed. Now, it's my time. No longer will I put everyone else before me. My phone beeps, letting me know my driver has arrived. One last look around and I'm finally starting my big adventure!

I keep looking at my tickets and my itinerary, not really paying much attention to the traffic. When I finally look up, we are no longer on the highway. "Where are we?"

"There was an accident and we were re-routed. Don't worry, we have plenty of time."

I pull out my phone and take care of some last minute emails I need to do for work. I quickly call my assistant Sidney and begin to give her some last minute notes on her voice mail. The car stops short, my phone flies out of my hands and lands at my feet. As I reach for it, the back doors fly open. Two men come in with guns drawn on me. "What do you want?" One of the men reaches down and grabs my phone off the floor and presses end.

I push my purse towards one of them. "Take it, please; I won't fight you."

"We don't want your purse. Stay calm and you might make it out of this alive."

My heart is beating so fast and the sweat begins to bead on my brow. I can hear the blood pounding in my head.

"Now, where is *it*?"

He runs the muzzle of his gun down my cheek. I clench my jaw to stop my teeth from chattering. I take a deep breath and whisper "Where is what?"

"Emerson left *it* behind. He hid it and we want *it*. We know you know, so don't bullshit us."

Realization hits and I'm sure my face just gave it away. I glance at my driver in the rear view mirror. He removes his hat and his glasses. He turns around and his stare sends shivers down my spine. I know I've seen him before. I'm usually good at placing faces but I can't place his. "I don't know what you're talking about. The only thing Emerson left behind is a lot of debt."

In an instant, I feel the cold butt of the gun slam against the side of my head. My world starts spinning into darkness.

FITZ

Today has flown by and nothing has been accomplished. Hudson was able to set up a lunch date with Ruby for tomorrow, so that's a plus. Sal has been working on the letter I sent him, but . . . still nothing. I glance at the clock and do the math in my head, Gail should be well on her way, if not there already. She is such a sweet lady and I wish she would put herself out there. I've never understood why she's never tried. Apparently, she's got reasons that I'm just not privy to.

> Me: Hey, Bailey, quick question. Did Emerson ever talk to you about cryptology?
> Bailey: He loved it. He would take ordinary papers and make them into something special that he would have Collin try to decipher. Is that important?
> Me: Yes, very important. I have something that I need Collin to decipher.
> Bailey: He's only ten years old. I don't want him involved.
> Me: I understand that but Emerson made him involved.
> Bailey: I need to be there when you have him look at whatever it is. If I think it's too much for him, then I will shut it down right there. Do you understand?
> Me: Yes, when can I see him?
> Bailey: Tomorrow, after school; he has a lacrosse game. He should be home by five.
> Me: Thank you. I'll see you then.

I go in the back to look for Sal and I find him still glued to the computer screen. Hudson came back after school. She has papers spread out all over the floor.

"Hey, guys, I think we might have caught a break. Emerson used to turn some papers into his secret code and have his son Collin decipher it. Bailey agreed to let me talk to him tomorrow."

"Well, I've gone through every file and there is nothing out of the ordinary. He did a lot of pro bono work and it was always criminal, never divorce. I looked through his banking records and he was borrowing from Peter to pay Paul for years. Then, when Lilly was born, he started spending like a drunken sailor. That's probably when the blackmail started."

She begins putting all the files back in the boxes while Sal pulls up Jake Daniels on his computer. His cases are endless, which is what I expected.

"Fitz, do you think he's in on this?"

"Whatever *this* is, no. So far, nothing is leading us down that path. Let's call it a night and we can pick this up again in the morning."

We all agree to meet back here tomorrow at ten. They head out to dinner and I go to Andy's house to spend time with my family.

CHAPTER
THIRTEEN

I OPEN MY EYES TO find the morning sun peeking through the blinds. The house is very quiet. The only thing I hear is the soft breathing from MJ. I'm spooned up against her back and she has my arms pulled tightly around her. I look over at the monitor, yep Patrick is still out cold. Maybe he's getting the idea that Mommy and Daddy need some morning time. I start by feather kissing up and down her neck. She lets out a little moan that makes my cock spring to life.

I slide my hand over her breasts and give her nipples a little tweak before I glide my fingers down her side. I stop at her tat just for a second and trace my finger around the Superman. God, I love her. I follow my fingers with kisses. Her skin is like velvet and always smells like vanilla and Cinnabons. I keep kissing her until she begins to wake up and slowly rolls on to her back. My non-stop kisses are everywhere. "Good morning, beautiful."

"What a wonderful way to wake up." She glances at the monitor and smiles.

"Don't worry, he's still asleep."

"How did you manage that?"

I kiss the inside of her leg and nip a little. "I had a chat with him. I explained if he wants a brother or sister then he needs to help me out."

She sits up, slips her arms under mine and pulls me up toward her. Her sweet lips on mine the entire time. Our tongues do a dance like leaves flickering in the wind. She pulls back, her green eyes are so bright and she gently runs her hand down my cheek.

"I would love to have another baby."

"Wrap yourself around me, babe."

I kiss her and slowly enter her. Slow, steady, buried so deep that it feels like we are one. My heart is racing to the finish line but my mind wants to slow down. "Oh, MJ, if only . . ." I pull my hips back and then slowly push forward.

"If only what?"

"You know."

"I do?"

"Yep, you know if only we could stay in this moment for a lifetime."

She sinks her teeth into my shoulder and I lose all my control. She's pulling me closer and I'm riding the wave of lost control.

I roll over and now with her on top of me, she takes control. Her beautiful ginger hair is everywhere as she takes me. The slow and easy morning pace has changed and now it's a hot frenzy.

"Fitz!"

"I'm right there with you, babe."

That's all it took. My name on her lips is what sends my heart racing time and time again. The only noise in the room is our hearts beating. I'm holding her tight as I try to catch my breath. She's sprawled across my chest, and I mindlessly stroke my fingers up and down her back. I'm just falling back to sleep when my phone rings with a familiar tone, one I haven't heard in a few months—Captain Hart.

"Hey, long time no hear, what's wrong?" At this hour, I know something is not right.

"I know you are no longer on the job, but I knew you would want to know—Gail is missing."

I sit up and rub my eyes, trying to clear away the fog. Maybe I didn't hear him right. "What do you mean, missing? She was on her way to Paris. I have her itinerary."

MJ moves off of me and I leap out of bed.

"She never made it."

"Damn it!" I yell. MJ begins tossing me some clothes. I'm trying to put them on without breaking my neck. "I want in," I demand.

"I won't fight you on this. I'm on my way to her house. I remember she said you put in an elaborate alarm system. What do I need to know?"

"I have a key, I'll meet you there."

"Okay."

I quickly clean up and, before I race out the door, I pull MJ in a hug. "I love you. I'll keep you posted."

I hop on Wanda and look up to see MJ by the window, waving. I drive off.

This early in the morning, everyone is heading into the city, so traffic heading out to the Island is light. I probably broke all kinds of speed records getting here. When I pull up, Hart is already there with a team. "Hey, now tell me everything."

"She was in the middle of leaving some instructions for her new assistant, Sidney, when it happened. I have the recording, you can listen for yourself."

He passes me his phone and hits play. I hear Gail's panic filled voice, one line, "*What do you want?*"

"That's it?! Did you check with the airline to make sure she didn't change her flight or something?"

"Fitz, this isn't my first rodeo. I checked; she never got on that plane or any plane for that matter. Her passport was not scanned, so she never left the country."

"Let's go inside." I unlock the door and disarm the alarm. Hart is treating it like a crime scene. We put on booties and gloves. There is not a pin out of place. I take my time and go through each room. It feels weird, like I'm invading her privacy.

"Do you think it has something to do with one of the cases she was working on?"

"I'm having Sidney pull every thing Gail had pending. But, I don't think she was working on anything that was high profile. Besides, she pretty much cleared up her work schedule for the next two weeks. I'm surprised you didn't put any camera's outside the house."

"I did, they are hidden. They are on a twenty-four hour loop. At midnight it downloads to the computer where it's stored for seven days. She's got an office in one of the bedrooms. If she didn't change the password on her computer, then I can get in."

The office is spotless like the rest of the house. The computer sits on an old rolltop desk. I power it up. "Damn it, she changed the password."

"Sidney said Gail sometimes does her paperwork remotely. Even if you get into her computer, you'll still need her work password to look at her pending cases."

I begin tearing apart her office . . . nothing. Think, Fitz, think like Gail. I close my eyes and take a deep breath. "I got it!"

"Got what?"

"She would have all her passwords in a book and a second copy on her phone."

One entire wall is filled with books. While Hart is going through all of them I search all the little cubbies in the desk. Finally the last one proves to be the winner.

"I got it!"

He pulls a chair up to mine. "We can start with yesterday and work our way backwards."

A nondescript town car backs into the driveway. A reflective plate cover hides the license plate. The driver gets out and puts her suitcase in the trunk. He has on a baseball hat and sunglasses. He looks to be about 5'10. He has some hair coming out from under his hat and it's dark.

"Not much to go on. Are there any other angles to this?"

"Yeah, hold on."

I pull up the footage from the other cameras. The screen fills with all different angles and photos from the entire perimeter.

"Jesus, how many cameras did you put out there?"

"She is a woman—alone. Apparently, not enough."

One of the cameras is able to get a shot of the driver sitting in his car. The time stamp is an hour before he pulls into her driveway.

"He was sitting in wait. Back up a couple of days."

I back up five days. Bailey shows up followed by me.

"Why where you here?"

"She asked me to help her friend."

"Fitz, with what? Right now, we have nothing so anything you could add to this might help."

While the footage runs, I fill him in on what's going on. "Maybe we can get something from the car she ordered. There has to be some sort of confirmation."

I pull up her emails and of course Gail has everything in folders. I open the Paris folder and I find the confirmation for the town car she ordered. While I look around some more, Hart calls the company. They inform him that she canceled the car.

"How could that be, we saw the car show up?"

"There is a cancelation in the deleted emails. If she really cancelled the car, the deleted email would have been stored in the

Paris folder."

"How is that even possible that it was canceled without her knowledge?"

"Maybe someone hacked into her computer or phone. Send everything to Travis maybe he can shed some light on this."

"Fitz, what the hell did she get herself into?"

"The bigger question is what the hell did Emerson get himself into? I'd bet donuts to dollars it's tied to him."

"Are you sure this Bailey lady has no idea as to what's going on?"

"Yeah, I'm sure. And if they think Gail knows, then they are going to assume Bailey knows, too." The words are barely out of my mouth and I'm racing out of the room.

"Where are you going?"

"I've got to get to Bailey and the kids before anyone else does!"

Thankfully, Bailey's house is only ten minutes down the road from Gail's. It's early enough that when I pull into the driveway, the kids are heading out the front door. Regina pulls up assumedly driving the kids to school. I block their path to the car and the older daughter is giving me the stink eye. You have not experienced life to the fullest until you've had a teenager give you the stink eye.

"Hi, kids, I'm Fitz, a friend of your mom's. There's no school today. Let's head back inside." They are looking at me and no one is moving. Regina begins beeping her horn, which brings Bailey out of the house.

"Fitz, what's going on here? The kids have to get to school."

"Why don't we take this inside and I can explain." I lock eyes with Bailey and I hope my intense stare and the fact that I'm blocking the walkway alerts her that I mean business.

"Kids, go inside while I let Regina know she doesn't need to do the car pool today. I'll be right in."

The kids grumble a lot but then head inside. The oldest one is still glaring at me. While I wait in the driveway for her to get rid of Regina, I look down and realize I still have on the booties. I quickly pull them off and call Hudson. No answer, damn it! Next, I try Dad, cuz, let's face it, he'll always answer the phone.

"Hey, Dad is Hudson there?"

"Little bit early for you to start tracking her down. She's here, we're having our morning coffee and discussing the news of the day. Hold on."

News of the day my ass, Dad is checking the ponies.

"Hey, Fitz, what's wrong?"

"Gail's been kidnapped. I'm already convinced it has something to do with Emerson. I'm at Bailey's house now. I'm having her kids stay home. Get in touch with Lucas and have him put some people on Bailey and the kids. I'll instruct them to stay put. When you go to meet Ruby, make sure you take Sal with you. Don't go alone!"

"Yeah, yeah. I don't think she's going to be a problem."

"Hudson, I'm not joking. Don't make light of this."

"Yes, now I need to go, if I'm going to get this done."

She hangs up without even a goodbye. This is what I have to look forward to. Regina drives away as Bailey heads back up the driveway.

"What did you tell her?"

"Not much because I don't know anything. The other day when you left, she asked who you were. She made a remark about me dating. Gail told her that you were her friend and you were installing a security system for me. Now, what the hell is going on?"

"Gail's been kidnapped. They probably think she knows where Emerson was hiding all of the stuff he had on them. If they think she has it or knows about it, then it's safe to say they think you know, too. They probably figured Gail would be an easy mark to get the information from. She's not—far from it. I don't want you or the kids to leave this house. I've ordered a security detail for all of you. Now, let's go inside and I'll explain it to the kids."

"Wait! Exactly what are you going to tell them? I don't want them to think their father was a bad man. And I sure as shit don't want them to know about Megan right now."

"I'm not going to spill the beans about Megan. After reading that letter, for what it's worth, I believe your husband was set up. Now, for what purpose—I have no idea, but we can tell the kids that until we can get their fathers affairs in order, they need to stay home. You can have their teachers email you their work, so they don't fall behind. Trust me, it's better than having someone going with them every where they go."

"What about Gail?"

"I will find her no matter what. Failure is not an option. It never is."

She quickly turns away to wipe her tears, as if I wouldn't notice. "Don't you think we should call the police and tell them everything we know?"

"They are already aware and on the case. Gail's kidnapping was the game changer. Not only are the police involved but so are the FBI."

"I'm not letting my kids anywhere near Regina."

"I agree. Now, let's get inside; it's cold and I need to explain to your kids what's going on. Besides, I don't want you hanging around out here."

Before I'm even in the door, my phone beeps with a text from Lucas alerting me that a crew is on their way.

CHAPTER FOURTEEN

Gail

OPEN MY EYES; EVERYTHING is blurry. I try to force myself to focus on my surroundings but my head is pounding. I feel the side of my head, and wince from the sharp pain. When my eyes can finally focus, I look around, trying to figure out where I am. The only thing I'm able to figure out is that I'm on a cold concrete floor in what looks to be an old warehouse. I try to move, but between the heavy chains I'm bound with and my pounding head, I just can't do it. I close my eyes and give in to sleep.

After a while, I try to open my eyes again. I don't know how long I've been here, wherever here is. Time keeps slipping away from me. I know on Tuesday I was on my way to Paris. That seems like a lifetime ago. I keep replaying in my head everything that happened. It's like a movie reel on a continuous loop. I hear footsteps and out of the shadows steps the man that was driving me to the airport. He looks familiar but, again, I can't place him. The more I think about it, the more my head hurts.

"Where am I?" I'm barely able to whisper. My mouth is so dry.

"Where you need to be for now. Where is *it*?"

There's that *it* again. The only thing I can think of is they want that paper that Bailey found. "Maybe if you told me what *it* is, I might be able to help you."

"I know you found it. That's why you called in your friend—*Fitz*." He practically spits out Fitz's name.

"I have no clue what you're talking about."

He steps in closer, invading my space. I'm trying to push down the fear that's creeping into my throat. He squats down, wraps his hand around my throat, and lifts me up from the floor. He pins me up against the concrete wall. I can't breathe . . .

"You can hold out if you want. You might not care about your own life, but what about the life of your friend Fitz? What about Bailey and her children? Trust me, I have no problem killing all of them."

His grip loosens a little and he steps in closer. His face now only inches away from mine.

"Why me? I mean if you have no problem killing everyone, why me? I'm a nobody who knows nothing!"

"You were an easy mark. The easiest of all of them. So, ask yourself this, Gail, will you be the first to crack or the first to die?"

He releases his grip from my throat and I fall to the floor. He turns to leave as it finally hits me who he is—Mateo, Regina's brother. I only met him once. I usually never forget a face but he has a scar now that he didn't have before. That's what was throwing me off. "Mateo, I don't have anything."

He stops, turns back around and kicks me in the ribs. Knocking the wind out of me.

"You just sealed your fate, bitch." And with that, he leaves.

I curl up into a ball and begin to pray. My head is pounding and I'm finding it hard to catch my breath. I can only hope Fitz knows what's going on and he's able to find me.

FITZ

Bailey's kids were not to happy that they were as they put it "under house arrest."

Sal is on his way over with everything he could find out from Emerson's computer. Hopefully I can get a beat on Gail and this will come to a quick ending.

> **Hudson: Hey, I got stuck in school and I had to change my meeting with Ruby. Sal is already on his way to you and by the time he comes back to get me, it will be too late. I really don't think it's a big deal if I go myself. After all, I'm a big girl and can take care of myself.**
>
> **Me: Hell no! Change the meeting with Ruby.**
>
> **Hudson: I already changed it once. She will get annoyed.**
>
> **Me: I don't care. Absolutely not!**
>
> **Hudson: Fitz, you are being unreasonable!**
>
> **Me: Unreasonable would be if I called Dad and told him what you want to do. We already have one person missing. I don't need to add you to the list. Call Lucas and he will have someone go with you. Safety in numbers.**

The one person she will always listen to is my dad. She respects him. He's never given her bad advice and if I have to pull that card out, I will. Safety before anything else.

> **Hudson: Unreasonable butt head. I'll call now.**

Just once, I wish everyone would stop fighting me on everything. Whenever there is danger, the women around me push back. I'm not a bad guy, just slightly neurotic.

I find Bailey in the kitchen with the kids. She's been cooking and baking all day while the kids are working on their homework. Whatever she's making smells damn good and my rumbling stomach reminds me I've had nothing to eat all day. I head in there to see if I can snag something but then Sad Sack starts his crazy spinning and barking.

"Bailey, I'll get the door. It's probably Sal." By the time I get to the door, the dog is totally out of control. I look out and see Sal heading up the walkway. I try to hold the dog back and let him in.

"Hey, I think for the most part, he's friendly."

Sal's a big guy. He squats down and slowly puts his hand out for the dog to sniff. He seems excepting of him and once Sal scratches behind his ears, he's got a friend for life.

"What's his name?"

"Sad Sack, don't ask."

He laughs, gets up and we head into the kitchen. As I introduce him to everyone, my stomach rumbles again and Bailey laughs.

"Fitz, I'll take that as a sign you want something to eat. Sal would you like something to eat or drink?"

"Yes to both, please. So, Collin, tell me how you and your dad got into cryptography."

He shrugs his shoulders. I want to step in but I think one on one with Sal will help the kid open up more rather then feeling like he's getting ganged up on.

"I don't know, we just did."

"My grandfather got me into it. He was in World War II and his job was in intelligence. He was only one of many that tried to decode German messages that were sent using a special machine called the Enigma Typewriter. He would tell me all kinds of stories about his time during the war. He would give me things to decode and he would always try to trick me. Did your dad do that with you?"

The kids face lights up and it looks like Sal found his way in.

"Yeah, he would hide stuff all the time and the only way I would be able to find it is by decoding his clues. But, he was constantly changing the code. Sometimes it would take me weeks to figure it out."

Shit, Gail doesn't have weeks. I'm about to freak out but then Sal reaches into his pocket, pulls out a paper and passes it to Collin.

"Do you think you can take a look at this for me. Your dad left some instructions for your mom to carry out, but I can't break the code. I guess he figured you could unscramble it all for her."

That's good, Sal, make him feel like he's needed. He's staring at it for a bit, then pulls a pad out of his backpack and begins making notes. We are all quiet and staring at him. *No pressure, kid.*

"I'll mess with it."

He puts on his ear buds and leaves the room! Damn it. I motion for Sal to walk me out. I don't want the kids to hear anything.

"Sal, I think while he works on it with you, I'm going to pay Jake Daniels a visit and find out everything he knows."

"What about Regina?"

"Captain has someone watching her. If we're lucky, she might lead us to Gail."

"Okay, I'll keep at it with Collin. Let me know what happens." He looks at his watch for the fourth time since he got here.

"Don't worry, Lucas sent someone with her. Hudson is tough."

I grab my sandwich and head out before he realizes I'm just as worried about her as he is.

CHAPTER
FIFTEEN

Hudson

M Y PROFESSOR WAS A BEAR today. One more year to go before I take the bar. That is—if I take the bar. Truth be told, I've been eyeing a career in law enforcement. I already took the police test, but only Sal knows, and I've sworn him to secrecy. Besides, I don't even know if I passed it yet. But, that's a story for another day. Right now, my focus needs to be on Ruby and getting Gail back alive. The longer they have her, the lower her chances are. Lucas sent the new guy, Tito, the biggest, meanest looking guy he has on the payroll. Unfortunately, that will not help me out with Ruby. I think Fitz intimidated her. He can do that. I know . . . I've experienced it first hand. Maybe I can convince Tito to give me some space.

"Tito, when I go in to talk to her, can you wait outside? I don't want her to feel overwhelmed by us." Maybe if I make it about us and not him I'll stand a chance.

"I'm sorry, Hudson, I have orders to follow and that's not going to work. How about if I take a seat at the bar and wait there for you?"

"Okay, I need her to feel comfortable talking to me. I need to find out if she knows anything that could help us find Gail." I throw out the guilt but he's not budging.

We head into the restaurant. Tito quickly goes to the bar, taking a seat that gives him a view of the front door. I take a table near the window that gives him a direct line of sight, so he can keep an eye on both of us.

She's late. I hope she's not standing me up. I must have checked my phone a million times, hoping she's not canceling. Finally, I see her round the corner. She sees me and waves. At the same time, a car comes barreling down the street. It swerves up onto the sidewalk, hits her, and keeps going. Tito and I are racing out the door to help her. It's bad; blood is everywhere. Her left leg is mangled and she is not breathing. "Call *911!*" I yell. Tito already has his phone out. I begin to perform CPR. After several minutes, I can finally hear sirens getting louder. It feels like forever until EMS shows up and takes over. I step back and wait while they try everything, but she never comes to. Tito pulls me back, his grip tight on my shoulders. My hands are covered in blood. I can't stop staring at them. The adrenaline kicks in and I can feel my body begin to shake. I can't stop it. I keep wiping my hands on my shirt but there is so much blood. I can't take my eyes off of my hands.

"Come on, Hudson, look away. You did everything you could." He tries to lead me away from the scene, but a police officer stops us.

"Ma'am, I need your contact information and exactly what happened here."

I open my mouth to speak and nothing comes out.

Tito pulls me behind him, sheltering me from everything. "We gave the other officer our contact information and told him what we saw. A car, that never even tried to slow down, hit the woman. We didn't see the driver or what kind of car it was. By the time we got outside, the car was gone."

Why is he lying to the cop? We saw the car as it was speeding away. I try to step around him but he makes it impossible. The cop turns to speak to the other bystanders and in one swift move he has me out of there.

"Why did you lie?"

"Shut up and walk, now!"

"But"

"Stop talking! We need to get out of here, fast!"

For the first time tonight, he looks worried. He's sweating and he keeps looking over his shoulder. He pulls me into an alley and we cut through yet another building before we double back to our car. He's got me pulled into a doorway a few doors down from where he's parked. His back to my front. He's so large that no one will be able to see me behind him. He's texting someone and when I step to the side and peer around him. I can make out it's Lucas. He's also loading the video. He finally turns toward me and puts his hand over my mouth. With his finger over his lips, he shushes me. I nod yes; he removes his hand and points to our car. Then, he pulls out his keys, steps out of the doorway, looks around before motioning me to follow behind him. He hits the remote and the car explodes. Shrapnel flies everywhere. In an instant, he turns and shields my body, but then he's hit in the back hard, knocking me down. He lands on top of me. Everything happened so fast.

"Tito!"

Our eyes lock and I crawl out from under him. When I look down to see where he is hurt, I can't hide my shock. Blood is pouring out of him and even though I know there is no saving him, I have to try. There is so much blood and I try to push it away to see if I can figure out where it's coming from. "Stay calm, Tito, I'll get help."

He grabs my wrist his grip is so tight. I'm not sure what to do, but then he pulls me close to him. "Take my phone, Run!" His voice is barely above a whisper. His hand falls away from mine and he's gone.

Sirens are getting louder. I crawl around, trying to find his phone. It was in his hand when the blast happened. Finally, I find it a few feet away, pick it up and run like the devil is breathing down my neck. I know my life depends upon it. I cut back through the ally but I'm not familiar with this part of Queens. For all I know, I could be running in circles, heading right into the arms of whoever planted that bomb. I finally find a subway station and hop on the first train that pulls into the stop. I'm underground, so I have no service. This time of night, there aren't a lot of people on the train, yet everyone is moving away from me. I look down and realize why. I'm covered in blood . . . shit! I turn away from the prying eyes, get up and head into the next car. The first stop I get to, I'm out of here. We begin to ascend on to the Queensboro Bridge, heading into Manhattan. I huddle near the door and as soon as the train gets into the Lexington Ave. station, the doors open and I run out.

I want to hail a cab but no one will stop with me looking like this. I find a guy selling sweatshirts on the street corner. I put it over what I'm wearing and hail a cab. Finally, one stops. I keep the hood down low, trying to hide my face. I head to the place I know I'm always safe—home. Thankfully, I have enough cash to pay the driver, so I won't leave a paper trail.

I take the steps two at a time. Racing towards the blasting TV. I know that's where Pat will be. When I get into the room, I drop to my knees and begin to cry. He wheels over to me and tries to pull me closer to him.

"Annie, hurry up! Something's wrong with Hudson, hurry!"

She races in and drops to the floor next to me. "Where are you hurt? Where is all this blood coming from? Dear God, is it Fitz?!"

"No, It's not mine or Fitz's. Someone killed Ruby and then Tito." I'm shaking and I can't stop.

"Annie, wrap her up in blankets. We need to keep her warm."

"Warm! You told me she was safe. She was going to be working in the office. Patrick, by all the saints above, she's covered in blood. That's not office work!"

"Hush up, I need to call Fitz."

She keeps a basket by the couch with all different blankets in it. She wraps me up and rocks me in her arms. I can't get the pictures out of my head. I can vaguely hear Pat on the phone. My teeth are chattering so loudly and my ears are still ringing from the blast. Everything sounds like a bad noise machine.

I'm not sure how long I've been wrapped up in the safety of Annie's arms but Fitz comes charging in like a bull.

"Mom, I've got her. Turn on the shower and make the water very hot." He bends down and scoops me up off the floor as Annie heads upstairs. "Listen to me, Hudson. I've got you and you're safe. No one can get to you here."

The teeth chattering is beginning to slow down but then Lucas comes through the door with MJ right behind him. How do I explain to him what happened? I keep seeing Tito's face, still trying to protect me to the very end. Is any of this my fault? Did I do something wrong?

"Fitz, bring her into the bathroom. I'll take care of her." MJ is always calm and strong. I wish I could be more like her. When we get upstairs, she pushes Fitz out the door. She passes me a small glass.

"First drink that. It will help with the chattering teeth."

I feel the burn of the Irish whiskey and my eyes begin to water. "MJ, they're dead."

"Shh, we can figure out what happened later. Right now, I'm going to get you undressed and into the shower."

She moves about in silence, like this is second nature to her. She helps me into the shower and then bags up all my clothes. She washes me like she's washing a child and right now, I wish I could be a little girl again. I wrap my arms around myself and give into the tears. . The water is getting cold. When I finally look up, MJ has a towel open for me.

"Are you ready to talk about what happened?"

"Everything happened so fast." I quickly wipe away the tears that are starting to fall.

"Okay, let's get dried off. Fitz is going to want to hear everything."

"Will you stay with me?" She's become the big sister I never had.

"You couldn't drag me away. Now, let's get dressed."

I open the door to find Fitz sitting on the floor. He jumps up and pulls me into his arms. "You will never fight me on the things I tell you to do . . . ever." His grip on me is like iron. I don't want to fight with him. Right now, I'm happy to know I'm safe.

"Fitz, she needs to breathe; loosen your grip."

He has his arms around both of us as we head downstairs. Lucas is pacing around the room like a caged animal. When he sees me, he stops and opens his arms. These guys are my family and when one hurts, we all hurt.

"Jesus, Mary, and Joseph, do you know how much you scared us? Sit down and tell me everything that happened."

Part of me wants to block it all out and never think about it again. However, I have a job to do and that job includes remembering every little detail. Gail's safety depends upon it. I go through it all while Lucas writes everything down. He hates technology and would rather have a pad and pencil. Fitz doesn't take any notes. Everything is in his head and that, in itself, is a very scary place. Sal is the tech wizard in the trio, always putting everything in his phone.

I realize he isn't here, which is unusual. "Fitz, did you tell Sal what happened?"

"I got a hold of him while you were upstairs. I promised him you were safe. He's working on that paper with Emerson's son. Who picked the place to meet Ruby?"

"When I first made the plans with her, I picked the place. After I had to change the plans, she picked the place. Lucas what did Tito send you?"

"What do you mean, he never sent me anything."

"He did!"

Lucas pulls out his phone and turns it towards me. Look this is the last message that I got. He said you were both inside the restaurant waiting for Ruby to show."

Now I think I'm losing my mind. MJ takes both my hands in hers.

"Close your eyes and replay what Tito was doing. Play it back in slow motion." Her voice is soothing.

I'm replaying everything and that's when it hits me. "He was in the middle of attaching a video to a text message when he stopped and put his hand over my mouth to shut me up. He turned and hit the car remote for the doors. He never had a chance to send it, that's why he said to take his phone and run. I have his phone, it's in the bag with my clothes."

MJ gets it out and passes it to Lucas.

"The phone is locked but this is the reason why we have each other's passwords. The screen is shattered but I can still pull up what he was sending me."

"I can't imagine what he saw. By the time we got outside, the car was already heading away from us and then it turned the corner."

"He must have seen something that made him record because he is scanning the crowd of bystanders."

Fitz takes the phone and replays it.

"Look at when he pans over the crowd. He stops on this one guy, and then the guy pulls his cap down and leaves. Maybe Tito recognized him?"

We are all huddled together replaying the video over and over again. Fitz tilts the phone towards me to give me a better look. "When Tito stops panning the crowd and focuses on the one guy, it almost seems like maybe the guy recognized Tito, too. Maybe that's why he lied to the cop and raced us out of there."

"Can we put Sal on this?"

"No, Lucas, I've got him working with the kid. I'll send it to Travis."

A few clicks later and Travis has the video. Lucas pulls Fitz aside.

"Where are you at with finding Gail?"

"I was headed to Jake Daniels office to see if he could shed some light on the letter that Emerson left with the lawyer when I got Dad's call. By now, he's probably home. I'll head over there and then back to Bailey's house to check on the progress."

"Okay, I'll stay here with Hudson until you get back."

The ringing in my ears is finally diminishing. All of a sudden there is a lot of commotion by the front door, which is not unusual in this house. But I think everyone is on such high alert that we all jump at the noise. The door flies open as Stella comes barreling in with Andy and Patrick behind her. I turn in time to catch her as she leaps into my arms. With her arms wrapped so tightly around me, I can hardly breathe. When she finally loosens her grip I lean back and see tears in her eyes.

"Hey, kiddo, what's wrong?"

She begins signing so fast I have a hard time keeping up. "Daddy said you were hurt. When people get hurt, they leave me."

"Andy! Why did you tell her I was hurt?"

In one very swift move, Annie smacks him in the back of the head.

"Mom, it's MJ's fault. She came over and I can't help it if Stella has gotten really good at lip reading."

I tap my finger to my lips and she focuses on me. "Stella, I'm fine. No one is going to hurt me or any of us, I promise."

That seems to satisfy her. She gives me another big hug before she slides out of my arms. She chases after Patrick. Fitz uses that as his cue to pull MJ and me aside.

"I'm going to head out, no one leaves this house, understood?" He directs his order at me. He doesn't wait for me to answer him cuz in reality, he's right. I wouldn't have a leg to stand on in a fight with him. Whoever put that bomb in Tito's car knew him and saw me. "MJ, walk me out, please." He gives Lucas a nod and with his arm around MJ, they head towards the front door. MJ is the rock of this family. She is the strongest woman I have ever met. This entire family relies on her for one thing or another and tonight just proves it. Once again, she will be the glue that holds us all together, no matter what, while Fitz goes off to save his little corner of the world. I've always wondered who MJ turns to?

CHAPTER SIXTEEN

Fitz

A S WE GET CLOSER TO the front door, my grip on MJ's waist gets tighter. This is the part I hate—leaving. When you're a cop, they can teach you everything except how to say goodbye. "Babe, I'm not sure how long I'm going to be gone for. Stay here at least until Lucas gets the security in place." I pull her close and nuzzle into the crook of her neck. I wish I could stay like this forever. She pulls back and kisses me hard before pulling away.

"I love you. Be safe and call when you can. Now, go be everyone's hero but just remember at the end of the day, you'll always be mine."

"God, I love you." I lean in and kiss her again. If I don't leave now, I never will. I head out and hop on Wanda. Looking back, she's on the top of the steps, her fingers on her lips. When she's finally out of sight, I really open it up. I've got to get to Jake's house. There's more to that letter—that's for sure.

Traffic is not so bad; before long, I'm in Long Island. The difference between the people that live on North Shore versus the South Shore of Long Island is as different as night and day. I was surprised that Gail purchased the house on the North Shore. She's more down to earth and not in to labels. Roslyn and Jake live about a mile away from Bailey. I guess the prosecutor's office is paying big bucks. The homes in Brookville are in the millions, and this one is right up there.

I walk up to the front door noticing all the cameras and spotlights coming on. Understandable, considering his job. I'm about to knock when a video screen by the side of the front door comes on. A very well-put-together lady comes on the screen.

"Can I help you?"

"I'm Fitzgerald Rodriguez, a friend of Bailey's. I would like to speak to Jake Daniels."

"Just a moment."

The screen goes blank. I'm about ready to start banging when the door opens and the lady from the screen is standing in front of me.

"I had to call Bailey and find out what was going on. Come inside." She opens the door and steps to the side. She's got a huge Rottweiler by her side.

"Nice dog. What's his name?"

"Thanks, it's Baxter. Now Bailey said you would be able to explain to me why she's locked up in her house and why you need to talk to my husband."

"I guess you went by there today." No one told me she stopped by.

"Yeah. . . You guessed right. I went there a little while ago to see if she needed anything and security turned me away. Now, what the hell is going on, and what do you want from me?"

"Actually, I would like to speak to your husband."

She is standing there with her arms crossed and a scowl on her face. She wants to come across as some hard ass, the only thing she is coming across as is rude. If I had the time, I would give her a dose of her own rudeness. Instead, I take a step closer, practically eliminating all of her personal space. I know how to be intimidating and look menacing. This is one of those times. I lean in so close, I can feel the heat coming off of her body. I lock eyes with her and her face begins to flush. She parts her lips and her breathing is becoming rapid.

At that moment, Baxter begins barking and bolts out of the vestibule.

"That would be my husband, so I guess you're in luck." She takes a step back and nearly trips over her own two feet. I can't help but smirk.

Jake Daniels steps into the room with Baxter at his heels. I've never testified in any of his cases but I heard he's tough. I extend my hand out to him. "Hi, I'm Fitz Rodriguez."

"Yes, I know who you are. Retired detective out of Brooklyn. Your reputation precedes you. What can I do for you?"

My gut tells me not to trust him . . . for that matter—both of them. These people are really starting to piss me off. They are so cut and dried.

"Well, can we maybe get out of the vestibule and I can explain to you what's going on." I'm usually never rude but I don't have time for this bullshit.

"Of course, but we need to make this quick. I've got a closing argument to work on. Let's discuss this in my office."

He leads the way with Roslyn following quickly behind me. I have to remind myself that Gail's life is at stake and I might need these people to get her back safely. He leads me into a home office and he takes a seat behind the desk. If he's trying to intimidate me, he's barking up the wrong tree. I take a seat directly across from him.

"Okay, now what can I do for you?" He looks down at his watch and back up at me.

"Well, Monday was the reading of Emerson Davis's will. As you already know, he was working on a plan to get out of the mess he apparently got himself into. He said you were helping him with that. Exactly what was he into?"

"I'm not at liberty to talk to you about it. I will, however, talk to Bailey if she needs something."

He's about to get up but I beat him to it. I slam my fist on the desk. I lean in so close I can see his jaw tick. "You will not cut me off. Gail O'Connor has been kidnapped because of this big cluster fuck of yours. I'm trying to find her. You need to tell me every damn thing you know—*now!*"

Roslyn grabs the corner of the desk. All the color drains from her face. However, Jake's face remains the same—emotionless.

"When did this happen?"

"Earlier tonight. Now, what do you know that might help me find her?"

After regaining her composure, Roslyn turns to leave. I quickly block her path.

"Where do you think you're going?"

"I'm going to call Bailey to find out if she needs anything, and Regina to let her know what's going on."

"Jake, you want to tell her why she can't do that or should I?"

He keeps looking from me to his wife. Finally, he gets up and puts his hands on her shoulders.

"Right now, Ro, for Gail's safety, it's best if we keep this information to ourselves." He conveniently leaves out that her douche bag friend is behind all of this.

"Okay, are we in any danger?"

"No. Can you give us a moment alone?"

If it were up to me, I wouldn't let her out of my sight. At the end of the day, I can't police everyone. She leaves and he resumes his position behind his desk. Maybe that's his extension of his dick. I don't give a royal fuck; I just want answers.

"Emerson never told me what he had, only that it would make my career. I do know whatever it was, he was blackmailed into it by Regina. He did tell me there are two separate keys he held. One is a link to a lot of money and the other is a link to some sort of ledger. Have they asked for any kind of ransom?"

"No, not yet. I have a crew set up at Bailey and Gail's house. I put security around Bailey and the kids. You might what to put someone on your wife." Just in case he decides to pull some shit, at least now he knows I've got coverage on everyone. The hair on the back of my neck stands up, a sure sign he's holding back. I pull out my business card and toss it on the desk.

"If you hear anything, call me. I can show myself out." I head out to find Roslyn waiting by the front door for me.

"Is Bailey okay?"

"What do you think?"

I don't wait for an answer. I slam the door behind me.

Roslyn

That man was really pissed and he has every right to be. Nothing is going the way it was planned and now Gail's in trouble. I look down the hall just as Jake comes out of his office.

"Ro, we need to talk."

"The time for talking has passed, Jake. This is a big fucked up mess and you could have stopped it a long time ago." I grab my bag and keys off the entryway table. Before I can reach for the door, he grabs me and spins me around. My bag and keys fall to the floor.

"I don't know where you think you're going, but you can't leave now. You're in this just as deep as I am. If I go down, you go down with me."

"I did what you asked. I betrayed my best friend. I went through all of Emerson's stuff and I found nothing. Now my other friend has been taken and God only knows what they are doing to her. All you can see is what Emerson dangled in front of you. Who knows if it's was even true? How many lives are you willing to risk so that you can get to the top?"

"Whatever it takes, Ro. The only reason you're here is to further my career. This has never been about love; I don't believe in it. All I believe in is me. But, you knew that going into this relationship and yet you still married me. You like the status you get from being my wife, so stop kidding yourself. I warned Emerson before he married Bailey not to do it. All he could do is spout out how he was so in love. That's where Emerson fucked up. He put feelings in the mix. Love is for fools, and that will never happen to me. I want nothing to complicate my life."

"After all these years, can you honestly stand there and say I'm nothing more than a whore in a skirt?!"

He cocks his head and raises his eyebrows. In that instant, I realize I hate him. I reach back and take a swing but he's faster then me. He ducks and in one swift move I'm face first, pinned up against the front door. My hair is fisted in his hand and his face only inches from mine. He sinks his teeth into my shoulder. I hear the telltale sound of his zipper and I know what's coming. This is nothing new with him. This is the only way he can get it up anymore. With one hand he pulls my skirt up and then rips my panties. In one swift move, he forces his cock inside of me. His fingers digging into my hip as he bites even harder. I close my eyes and mentally count to ten. I know that as fast as it started is as fast as it will end. One final push along with a few grunts and he's done. He backs up and when I turn around he's already putting his sorry excuse for a cock away.

"Now get cleaned up and get my dinner. It's going to be another long night."

I adjust my clothes and head into the bathroom to clean up from his brutality. He never leaves marks where anyone can see them. He leaves them on my heart and soul. He's made me into someone I hate, and the sad part is, I let him. Bailey always thinks that I'm the strong one. In reality, I'm the weakest of the four of us. A hard shell on the outside and a broken little girl on the inside.

CHAPTER
SEVENTEEN

FITZ

WITHIN TWO MINUTES, I'M BACK at Bailey's house. Sad Sack has given up greeting me, probably because Sal is mindlessly giving him yet another belly rub. Collin is curled up on the couch with the headset on. Hopefully, he's making progress. I'm not in the door two seconds and Sal is already pumping me for answers.

"Sal, she's fine, a little shook up, but fine."

His eyebrows draw together as if in disbelief. He takes a few breaths, probably in an effort to calm himself.

"Hey, what is it? You know you can talk to me about anything."

"She made me promise and you know I will take a secret to my grave, but this . . . I can't."

Jesus, what the hell? "Look, if it's something that could hurt her, then all bets are off and you have to tell me." I feel like Father O'Neil, giving absolution from sins.

"She took the police officers exam. That's why she had to change her appointment with Ruby. She said she is going to wait for her results before she said anything. Fitz, I don't think I could survive it. Hell, if this is any indication, then I know I can't."

I feel like I just got kicked in the gut. "Why would she do that? She's doing so good in law school. We need a lawyer in this family, not another cop!"

"She wants the adrenaline rush. She's tired of being buried with her head in a book."

"Maybe today scared her enough that she'll forget about all this nonsense."

"Do you really believe that?"

"No, but right now, I need something to hang my hopes on. In the meantime, I won't tell her I know about it. Let's just let it play out."

The thought of Hudson walking a beat sends a chill up my spine. I get a bottle of water from the fridge and take a moment to calm down. As much as I want to blame Sal for Hudson's decision, I can't. I blame myself. I agreed she could work at the agency. I'm the one who has her help with witnesses. I've involved her in everything. It's all on me. As much as I always tease her and tell her she's a pain in my ass, I love having her around. My parents love her like she's been a part of this family since the day she was born. As soon as this case is over, I'm going to talk her out of becoming a cop. For now, I need to focus on the here and now.

"Where are we at with the kid?"

"He's trying. I went through Emerson's office and he had some books about secret codes. I'm going through them, too. I made another copy of the letter that Travis gave me from Emerson's computer. I figured if we both worked on it, maybe we could come up with something. Have you found out anything from the video that Tito took?"

"No. I think he recognized someone in the crowd. Travis is working on it with Lucas. I went to Jake's house. Now there's a piece of shit, if I've ever seen one. I know he's hiding something."

My phone rings and it's Hart. I put it on speaker, so Sal can hear. "Hey, Captain, you're on speaker. Have you heard anything?"

"Yeah, a call came in on her house phone. Fitz, the voice was distorted but they asked for you. They said you have fifteen minutes to take their call otherwise, she's dead."

"I'm on my way." I hang up and race out the door.

In a matter of minutes, I'm back at Gail's house. The captain is waiting in the doorway for me.

"Lucky for us they all live in the same neighborhood. Were you able to get a trace or proof of life?"

"No, try and keep them talking as long as possible."

"Did you forget it's me you're talking to, Captain?"

"No, I'm just very nervous."

"You know they are going to be scrambling the call. The most we can hope for is proof of life," I mutter. He grunts and continues staring out the window.

While we wait, I take the time to look around. I don't understand why she's never met the right person. She has no baggage. No ex. No kids. Hell, she doesn't even have a pet. She's an only child and both her parents are gone. Highly educated, has a great job with a pension. Why hasn't someone swept her off her feet? I'm lost in my thoughts when I hear the phone ring.

"This is Fitz."

"Emerson had two things that belonged to us. Find them and you can get the girl back."

"What things?"

"A ledger and a partial key code. We know the ledger is encrypted. You need to find it, decipher it, and get everything to us within two hours. The clock is ticking."

"Wait! Two hours is not enough of time."

"Well, then you better hurry."

"I want proof of life or you get nothing."

In less than a minute my cell phone chimes and there is a video. "That's your proof. Tick tock, Fitz."

The line goes dead. I upload the video to Gail's computer. She is sitting on a wooden crate. It looks like she's in some sort of abandoned industrial type building. I hit play.

"Fitz, I'm sorry."

A masked man smacks her hard across the face. "Stick to the script."

She begins again. "This is your proof of life." She turns towards her captor and then back to the camera. "Don't do it, Fitz!"

In one swift move, he kicks her off the crate and the video goes black.

I try to rein in my temper, it will do no one any good right now. "Send this to Travis. See if he can pull something from the surroundings. I'm heading over to Bailey's house."

"What are you going to do? You don't have what they want."

"Put on my best poker face and bluff."

I leave him there to take care of things while I head to Bailey's house. Just as I walk in the door, Sal and Collin are giving each other high fives.

"Please tell me you've got something for me to run with."

"Collin was able to decipher the letter. Let's go into the office and I'll go over it all with you."

He must have a reason he wants to discuss this in private.

"Fitz, the letter explains what Emerson was doing. Once I saw how Collin was deciphering it, I took over. The kid is only ten and he doesn't need to know how fucked up his father was.

"Mateo and Regina created an app for sex. The client orders whatever type of sex they want. They secure their spot with a fifty thousand dollar bond. The kinkier the sex, the higher the cost. Emerson kept the bond money and made a ledger, documenting every person and corresponded it with what type of sex they ordered. He also made sure that every client's sexual encounter was filmed without their knowledge. Emerson attached the recording to the customers file. All of the money from each transaction went into an account. Mateo, Regina, and Emerson had a piece of the electronic key code and when they put all three pieces together, they are able to access the money. That paper Bailey found was Emerson's part of the key."

"Jesus, how do people even think this shit up?"

"That's not even the bad part."

"There's more?"

"Yeah, that's just the tip of the iceberg. Part of the money goes to Mateo's contact from China who supplies him with Fentanyl in it's purest form. He's supplying the entire eastern seaboard with the drug. And get this—he's using the post office to get the stuff into the states and shipped around. The dealers are cutting the Fentanyl with heroin and then putting it out on the street. They are creating their own version of China White. All the money goes back into the account and Mateo would pay his China contact from that account. He made sure Emerson was knee deep in it all. When Emerson found out about the drugs, he threatened to turn everything over to the police. That's probably where he brought Jake into the picture. If Mateo and Regina can't get access to the money, they can't pay Mateo's contact. That can be really bad for everyone. Are you sure Emerson died from natural causes?"

"Gail didn't do the autopsy since she was friends with him. She said she looked at the report and it was natural causes. She called it the widow maker, and the toxicology report came back clear. Where are the ledgers?"

"I haven't found them yet. What happened with Gail?"

"They gave me two hours to give them everything, including the deciphered ledgers. They beat her, Sal. I've got to give them something," I plead. He jumps back onto the computer. "Talk to me; what are you thinking?"

"We give them something, just not everything. Give them the key for the money, but I'll change a few things on it, so it won't work. Then we try to negotiate for the ledgers. I can create one fake page of a ledger but put it in the code that Emerson used. It will look similar to the key and that will at least buy us some time. They will think it's the real deal." A couple of keystrokes later and he prints out a page for me, along with the altered key code.

"Okay, I'll head back to Gail's house and wait for the call. Keep trying to find those ledgers!" I shout as I'm, once again, running out the door. I shove the paper in my boot before I rev up Wanda. I don't get very far down the road, when I notice in my mirror that I've picked up a tail, a bright red mustang. I mean, if you're going to tail someone, at least have the brains to pick a nondescript vehicle. I speed up and then take a few turns on to some different streets. It's easy to get lost out here and I'm hoping since it's dark, that will be the case. We are playing cat and mouse, and I keep hearing tick-tock in my head. I speed up a little bit more, just as a black town car blows the stop sign. I have no choice; I try to swerve to avoid it but in doing so, I spin around and hit the mustang head on. I'm flying in the air. It feels like everything is happening in slow motion. I can hear the screeching of the brakes and then the crunching of metal, which I pray to God is not Wanda. The smell of burning rubber fills the air. The minute I hit the ground, I'm surrounded. When I try to move, I'm hit with a Taser, causing my muscles instantly freeze. Finally, the Taser stops, but I'm dazed. *Come on Fitz, fight it off.* My mind says yes but my body is not listening. In an instant, one of the men cuffs me and tosses me into the back of the town car. Shots begin to ring out, and I'm trying to keep my head down, though I still don't have much control. Everything is happening so fast. The driver jumps back into the car and two men climb in the back with me. We speed out of the development and onto the main road. I pull myself up to look out the window. I'm trying to keep an eye out for landmarks, but then I feel a prick in my arm and I'm out.

CHAPTER EIGHTEEN

Lucas

I've taken up pacing and it's driving everyone crazy, myself included. Waiting has never been my strong suit. I need some air, maybe clear my mind a bit. I head downstairs. My phone beeps with a text:

Sal: Fitz never made it back to Gail's house.

Me: What do you mean he never made it back? Where is he?

I don't like the direction this is heading.

Sal: Hart called me. He said the police responded to a shooting around the corner from Gail's house. They found Wanda crushed under another vehicle. There are a couple of casualties, but no sign of Fitz.

Me: Did Hart have anything else?

Sal: No. Lucas . . .

Me: Stop right there. We can't assume anything. He's been in worse situations and survived. You need to stay focused.

Sal: I'm going to keep working on trying to locate the ledgers.

Now that I know the code, I'll decipher them. At least we will have some bargaining chips.

Me: I'll let the family know what is going on. Keep me posted.

Sal: Will do.

On a whim, I try his phone but it goes right to voice mail. I have to try to convince myself that what I told Sal is true. Fitz is a survivor. The hard part is telling his family. Every step upstairs feels like an eternity. When I step inside the room, Andy takes one look at me and pulls his mom into his arms.

"Lucas, what is it?" Andy asks with his mom tightly in his arms.

"Fitz is missing. Wanda was crushed by another vehicle. There were a few casualties but none of them Fitz. He's missing, I'm sorry; that's all I know. As soon as I find out anything, I will let everyone know."

Annie turns into Andy and begins to sob uncontrollably. Pat shuts the TV off, puts his head in his hands, and begins to cry. *"Not my boy, God, not my boy. Take me, but not my boy."*

Hudson tries to console him, but she's crying too. It's MJ I'm most worried about. She's quiet, watching Stella and Patrick play. Maybe she's in shock? I turn her towards me.

"MJ, did you hear what I said?"

"I heard you, Lucas. You fear he is dead, but I know he's not. My heart is still beating, so I'll always have hope. That same hope also fills me with fear. But you see, I know he's still alive, because without him, my life would be over. My hope is so much stronger than my fear."

They have a bond like nothing I've ever seen before, but there will come a point when she will have to face the truth, we all will. I pray to God I'm wrong and that day never comes.

"Do you have security in place for us yet? I would like to go home now."

"I do but wouldn't you rather stay here with your family?" I don't know why I ask; MJ does what MJ wants.

"Well, I would rather go home and wait for my husband."

Andy, with his mom still tightly in his arms, watches as MJ gathers up Patrick and gets ready to leave. She won't look at anyone as she quietly heads for the door.

"Andy, I don't think she should be alone."

"Let her go, Lucas. Right now, that's exactly what she needs."

Stubborn family. I notify the security team outside that she's on her way out. They are to take her home, do a sweep inside and out. They are to stay on her until further notice. Now, we wait.

MJ

Lucas must have half the agency's men and women watching me. I know he means well, but all I need is Fitz. I will not fall into a pity party. I know every wife or husband of a cop experiences this, it's their worst nightmare. When is goodbye really forever? I've had that fear long before we were ever married. Andy thinks I've come to terms with Fitz's job and the consequences. That couldn't be further from the truth. Every day I wish my husband had picked a different career path. However, at the end of the day, he's doing what he does best, helping people who can't help themselves. But, at what cost?

With Patrick fast asleep, the house becomes quiet again. It's the nighttime without him that I hate the most. I grab one of his many Superman t-shirts, put it on, and crawl into bed. I hug his pillow, like I do every night, and wait for him to come home. Tonight, however, I'm hugging it a little bit tighter. His smell is all around me, and I'm trying not to cry. But, the wall I've built up begins to crumble down to my soul. The damn of tears start and there is no way of stopping them. I bury my face into his pillow and pray. "Dear, God, I know you can hear me. Please, I can't do this without him. I need him, God, and I've never needed anyone like I need him. He makes my heart continue to beat. He is every breath I take. Every dream I have. Every laugh-out-loud moment I have is because of him. Our story is not finished . . . *Please*. Don't let it end like this." *Come back to me, Fitz. Come home, baby.*

Gail

There is a lot of yelling outside the door. I'm hoping it's going to be the police here to rescue me. Finally, the door opens with a bang and two men are dragging Fitz into the room. "Fitz! Fitz!" My screams are going unanswered and that's when I realize he's unconscious. He's not here to rescue me, no one is. They chain his arms like Jesus on the cross and take turns blasting him with a fire hose. I'm off of my crate, dragging my own damn chains behind me trying to get to him.

"Stop it, please! Leave him alone. I'll give you whatever you want, just leave him alone."

I hear him moan and then he finally lifts his head and his eyes meet mine. He looks at his chains and then around the room. Mateo comes into the room and grabs Fitz's hair, pulling his head back so he can see his face.

"Tell me, where the key and the ledgers are? If you tell me you just might make it out of here alive."

"Go fuck yourself."

"Not today," he growls out.

He walks over to a small table. There is a lot of stuff on it but I'm to far away to make out what any of it is, that is until I hear the crack of a whip. My heart sinks a little further as Mateo takes a few steps closer to Fitz. With every crack of the whip, Fitz's body jerks. I look away. I can't bear to watch. I put my hands over my ears, trying to drown out the sound of them whipping him. It doesn't help. All because he tried to save me, he can lose everything he holds dear. *I'm so sorry, Fitz.* I drop to my knees and scream *"stop"* over and over again.

When the whipping stops, I look up to find our captors leaving. Everyone, that is, except for Mateo. Fitz is on his knees, still chained, his body in a slumped position.

"Mateo, please leave him alone. I can get you whatever you want. You don't need to do this. He knows nothing."

"You are fool, Gail. Regina could never figure you out. None of your friends could. You hid your feelings well. That is, until now."

He takes a few steps closer and I can feel the panic rising in my throat. I've never said a word to anyone until I told Bailey the other day. He crouches down in front of me, close but not close enough.

"What do you want?"

"I want you the get Emerson's key and the ledgers from him. Do that and I'll let him live, and you can spend the rest of your days pining away for a love you'll never have."

I look past his shoulder and see Fitz lift his head. How much of that did he hear?

"I'll get them for you, if you let him go." His eyes lock with mine like he's searching for the truth.

"I showed you good faith when I gave you Fitz's cell number to send the video. I promise I'll get you everything."

"Tell me where they are and I'll get them. When I have it all, I'll let you both go."

"I don't know where Emerson hid them but give me some time

alone with Fitz and if he knows, I can find out."

He gets up, looks back at Fitz and then to me. I stand up and he takes a step closer. Just when I think that maybe he believes me, he swings his leg around and hits me square in the ribs knocking the wind out of me again. I hit the ground and curl up into a ball. This time, it hurts to even breathe.

"Do you think I'm some sort of idiot, Gail? Guess again. It will give me a thrill to watch you while I make him suffer."

I look over towards Fitz and one of the men is back in the room. He's pulling the chains, so Fitz's arms are stretched out as far as possible. Mateo walks over to the table, picks something up and steps up to Fitz. When he holds it up in the light, I can see it's some sort of shot. Fitz begins to kick and scream, trying to fight him off. One of the men ties off Fitz's arm. Mateo holds up the needle again. He looks over towards me and then sticks it in Fitz. It doesn't take long before whatever he gave him kicks in and the man releases the chains as Fitz's whole body slumps to the floor. They head to the door, but Mateo stops and turns towards me. "Watch him suffer, Gail. I will get him hooked and then hold back his next fix. I will make him beg, except he won't be begging for you." He laughs as he heads out the door.

When the door locks, Fitz's eyes fly open. He has a look of sheer terror, something I've never seen on him before. His head slumps forward again. I'm trying to crawl towards him but it hurts to breathe, let alone move.

"Take small, short breaths, Gail, it won't hurt as bad."

"Fitz, oh my God, Fitz, what did they give you?"

"If I had to hazard a guess: Fentanyl cut with heroin. But, that's a long story for another day. I need you to try and loosen these chains from the pulley system, so I can, at least, put my arms down."

I'm crawling and taking small breaths while dragging the long heavy chain behind me. I know I must have at least one bruised rib, along with a softball size lump on the side of my head. I can't stop; I have to help him.

"Gail, are you still here?"

"I'm here, Fitz. I'm trying to get to the chains. Hang on, please."

He begins to laugh.

"What the hell are you laughing about?"

"This is one fine mess we've gotten ourselves into."

Finally, I reach the chains and release the lever. He tumbles to the floor. When I finally make my way to him, he's in and out of it. I cradle him in my arms as best I can and pray that we make it out of here alive.

CHAPTER
NINETEEN

Andy

I FINALLY GOT STELLA TO bed at my mom's house. I wanted to stay close to Lucas in case he heard anything but right now, my sister needs me more. She is the strong one, the glue that has always kept this family together. I know she went home so she would be able to fall apart in the safety of her own home. But, she doesn't have to do it alone.

I cut through the alley with the security that Lucas put on me. When I get to MJ's house, I climb the steps, knowing that the house will light up like the Fourth of July. As much as the neighbors hate all the lights, they love all the security. When I open the door, I find MJ curled up on the floor at the bottom of the steps with a pillow and the baby monitor in her hand. The fact that she is wearing one of his shirts does not go unnoticed by me.

"What are you doing down here?"

"What do you think? I'm waiting for him, Andy. I'll always wait for him."

My heart is breaking, not just for her but for all of us.

"Has Lucas heard anything more?"

"You know I would tell you. There is no news."

"Tell Lucas I want Wanda. I'm going to repair it, so when he comes home she will be waiting for him."

I pull her into my arms and laugh. Even in the worst of times, she puts everyone else before herself. "You hate that bike."

"I really do, but I love Fitz more. That damn thing has been a bone of contention for us, but it's a part of him. I'm not joking, Andy, I want it back right away."

"Okay, calm down, I'll talk to Lucas about it later. Come on, let's go upstairs; it's almost dawn. I'll put up a pot of coffee. It's going to be a long day for all of us."

We head upstairs. It's time for me the big brother to support her for a change. "You know you can lean on me, sis, no matter what."

"I know but he'll be back, Andy."

I don't know if it's faith or if she is delusional. Hell, maybe it's a little of both. We curl up on the sofa and with the blinds open, we watch the sun come up. When the block is all lit up, she looks out the window and begins to shake.

Just like mom, MJ keeps a basket of blankets by the couch. Thinking she's cold I grab one and cover her. Then the tears begin to fall and I know she's not cold. She's got that empty feeling in the pit of her stomach. Looking out the window, Wanda is gone and no sign of Fitz. I pull her into my arms and rock her. The same way I did when she was just a little girl in love with a boy who would become her hero. Hell, I don't want to believe he is dead, but I also don't want to give her false hope.

"I'm here for you, MJ, always." All I can do is listen.

Sal

I checked in with Hart and he hasn't heard anything. He sent over the report from CSU, along with photos from the scene. It's pretty bad. Seeing Wanda under the mustang . . . I shudder at the sight of her mangled frame. Three men are dead, and the mustang is riddled with bullets. Why the shoot-out? Why take Fitz? Why not follow him since he's the one who can give you what you want? I have to many questions. I need help with some of this and know exactly who to turn to.

> **Me: I need your help. It's bad. Fitz is missing. I know he's in trouble and I don't know how to help him.**
>
> **Travis: Hart filled me in on everything he knows. I'm sitting here looking at the pictures from the scene. What do you need me to do?**

I quickly fill him in on everything we've discovered so far, including the drugs. I'm thinking maybe the DEA can help with that angle.

> **Me: Can you hack into Jake Daniels computer? Not the work one, the home one. Fitz had a bad feeling after he left there.**
>
> **Travis: I'm landing in 15 minutes. After I spoke to Hart, I called in some IOUs. I will have the weight of the bureau come down on Jake Daniels like nothing he's ever seen before. By the time I'm done with him, he won't know which end is up. I also did a trace on Fitz's phone—nothing.**
>
> **Me: I did too. It ends where they took him. Hart was going to find out if CSU came up with it. Did you get anything off of**

the video from Tito's phone?

Travis: Yeah, I ran it through a few different programs I have. Tito had a Juvie record. He was in a program called scared straight. The guy in the video is Angel Lopez. He was in the same program as Tito. Lopez recognized Tito, and my guess would be that's what got him killed. I'll bring the DEA up to speed on what you have so far. If they know anything, we can pool it together. Sal, Hudson needs to have protection on her until this is over.

Me: That's already taken care of. I'm glad you came. Is Olivia with you?

Travis: She wouldn't be anywhere else. MJ is going to need all of us around her for support. I'll let you know when we get to Jake Daniels's house.

Me: Okay, and thanks Travis.

Fitz has done so much for so many and has never asked for anything in return. Now he's in trouble, and everyone is coming to help.

I pulled up everything I could find on Jake. On paper, he's perfect. Fitz always says there is no such thing as a perfect person. Everyone is flawed. It's another reason to be excepting of everyone. I'm glad I asked Travis to look into Jake. I trust Fitz's gut; if he said there was something wrong, I believe him. In the meantime, if I could find these ledgers, I would have something to bargain with, along with the key for the money. Sad Sack lifts his head as Bailey comes in with coffee and a bagel.

"Thanks."

"It's me who should be thanking you. I know why you stopped Collin from deciphering the rest of the stuff. I appreciate all you're doing to protect my family. I feel bad. Because of us, two great people are in danger."

"Bailey, none of this was your fault. We'll find them. I'm not one to quit, and I have no problem asking for help. We'll get it done."

"Your girlfriend is very lucky. I'll let you get back to work."

I don't answer her cuz right now, the guilt is eating me up inside. I can't even work up the nerve to call Hudson. I shared her secret with Fitz. It wasn't my secret to share. She trusted me and I broke that trust. My tough guy side, as she calls it, won out over my logical side. I know there will be a price to pay, I just hope losing her won't be the cost.

I shake all these thoughts away and get back to the matter at hand: finding everyone. I'm stuck on one line at the bottom of the letter and it's really frustrating me. I stop scratching the dog and take a sip of coffee. He sits up and puts both his front paws in my lap. I run my hand under his collar and scratch. He begins thumping his paw and I can't help but laugh. I'm looking at his collar; he has so many tags attached to it. Maybe he has medical tags like my mom's dog. I begin looking at them and realize the answer was staring me right in the face the whole time! Sad Sack! I take his collar off and hold it up to the light.

"Bailey!" I scream for her.

She comes running through the door, nearly tripping over her own two feet. "What's wrong?"

"Tell me everything you know about the dog."

"Are you serious?! I'm a mother of three children and you're yelling like the world is coming to an end over the dog? You almost gave me a heart attack! What do you want to know?" She's bent over her hands on her knee's trying to catch her breath.

"I'm sorry. I didn't mean to scare you. Where did this dog come from?"

"He followed Emerson home one day and never left, why?"

I'm not ready to tell her anything else. I'm sure I can trust her but, then again, look at her friends. My mother always says *your friends are a reflection of you.* She also quotes *The Godfather,* "*Keep your friends close and your enemies closer.*" However, that's for another day. "I'm not sure, yet. What else can you tell me about the dog?"

"Sal, there is nothing to tell. He's a family pet."

"Do you have the passwords for Sad Sack's vet and licenses?"

"Emerson wrote them all down in case I needed them."

She goes in the desk and opens the top drawer. It's equivalent to everyone's standard junk drawer. She pulls out a card and passes it to me.

"That's the vet's card. On the back are the passwords for the vet and the microchip people. There is even one for Sad Sack's medical insurance. How is all of this helpful to finding Gail and Fitz?"

"A hunch. I'll let you know if I find anything."

I wait for her to leave the room and quickly pull up the website for animal microchips. All this time I've been thinking like me when I should have been thinking like Emerson. I punch in the user name and password, and there it is. I remember my mom had to put her dog Fredo's (there's that Godfather thing again) medical information on the account, along with phone numbers and stuff.

There is all the usual stuff and when I get to the part with phone numbers, the first two are Emerson's and Bailey's cell phone numbers. I scroll down further and there is a box for comments. That's where all the information sits. A series of numbers that to a layperson would mean nothing, but to Emerson, it's a gold mine. I hit print and log out. Next up, the actual tags that are on the collar. The yellow one is for the microchip. The red one is the rabies tag. There is one more with his name on the front and on the back, a series of numbers and letters that look nothing like phone numbers. Emerson hid everything in plain site. I look at the last line in the letter and using what I have, I'm able to determine that it says: With Sad Sack, everything is under his nose.

I take everything with me, including Emerson's laptop and head out to catch up with Travis and Hart. I think I know where the ledgers are. Right now, the best thing is safety in numbers.

CHAPTER
TWENTY

Jake

I T'S EARLY AND I'VE BEEN running on my treadmill for thirty minutes, trying to clear my head. I thought I was doing good, until the FBI came knocking on my door. They think they are scaring me; what a fucking joke. I've got my ace in the hole very well hidden, not even Ro knows.

They took our computers and phones. To say Ro was pissed is putting it mildly. At least she still has the house phone, so maybe she won't bitch too much. Lucky for me, I keep a burner phone in a false bottom in my car, along with my throw away .44. I was prepared for this. It took me twenty years to work my way up to top prosecutor in New York City. What do I have to show for that? Budget cuts, pay freeze and all the vacation time I accumulated put on hold. All the conservative organizations keep trying to convince me to run against de Blasio. The last thing I want is to be mayor of this city or even governor. I hate politics and most people. Well, except for me. Ro thinks I'm doing all of this to boost my name. What a fucking joke that is. Everyone who is anyone knows who I am. Right now, I want out. But, I'm not going out without being set for life. I plan on leaving her and this rat race life I'm living in behind.

Bailey threw a monkey wrench in my plans when she hired Fitz. He disrupted everything. He has a reputation of being a bull-dog when it comes to getting to the truth. Now, it's every man for himself.

"Jake, have you even heard anything I said?"

Her voice right now is like nails on a chalkboard.

"Yes, I heard you, Ro, I'm not going to the office today. I'm sure the FBI is there now, cleaning out all my stuff. They have every in-tention of crawling up my ass with a fine-tooth comb. That includes my office. You might want to prepare yourself cuz I'd bet a million buck that you're also on their list."

"I called out of work today, but I'm not sitting in the house with you all day. I'm going to try to go to Bailey's house."

She tries to leave, but I grab her arm, practically lifting her up off the ground. "You can't go anywhere without me. So don't even test me, Ro, not now." I let go of her and she stumbles backward, hit-ting the wall. I walk out, head down the hall into my office, and slam the door. Damn it! Fucking Fitz. I had people watching Bailey and Gail's house. When he took off from Bailey's, he had to have some-thing. Simple instructions, grab the guy off of his bike. How fucking hard could that be? Instead, there is a shoot out that is all over the news! Fitz was taken and the guys I hired were left for dead in the middle of the street. I grab my cup and fling it across the room. It hits the wall and shatters to pieces . . . third one this week.

When Emerson came to me for help, I saw my out. It was easy. Once I had the ledgers, videos, and everyone's code for the bank ac-count, I could leave the country. I set everything up for him and his family. The last fucking minute, Emerson got cold feet and wanted to back out. He wanted to just turn everything over to Mateo and

Regina and walk away. He thought his precious Bailey would be safer that way. I couldn't let that happen. And I, sure as shit, am not going to let Mateo get his hands on this stuff. I've worked too long for practically nothing. Now I'm riding that rainbow and the pot of gold is within my reach. Nothing is going to stand in my way.

I walk out of my office and I can hear Ro on the treadmill. I head down the hall and into the basement, locking the door behind me. I made sure to watch the FBI when they were down here. They never found it. It's so well hidden that Ro doesn't even know it exists. Besides, she only comes down here to set the laundry up for Louise, the housekeeper. I shut off the cameras that are all around the room. Finally, totally alone, I pick up the dummy television remote and with the press of a few buttons, one of the walls slides open, revealing a very well hidden, fully equipped panic room.

The door opens and he jumps up from his bed.

"Relax, Emerson, nothing has changed. Well, at least for you it hasn't. You're still my prisoner and to the world, you're still dead."

"Are you here to torment me again?"

"All of this could be avoided if you would just give me what I want. Now Mateo is holding two people prisoner. It's only a matter of time before he goes after your kids. Or your precious Bailey."

"Who does he have?"

"Don't worry. Like I said, it's not your family—at least—not yet. Right now, he has Gail and a former detective, Fitz. How much did you reveal in your will? Did you tell Bailey where everything is being kept? Is that why she hired Fitz?"

"I don't even know who that is! When I first came to you, I was prepared to give you all of it. Then Regina started threatening me again to tell Bailey about Megan. All I did was try to protect my family and now they are in a world of danger. If I give you everything, you'll kill me. If I hold out, they will kill my family."

"Well, you do have a point there, but look at it this way . . . to the world, you're already dead. Tell me where I can find everything, and I'll make this right for your family."

"You have no intention of keeping my family safe. You are only out for yourself, so go fuck yourself."

"Have it your way."

I turn to leave and I hear her gasp. She's standing there with her mouth hanging open and she begins to sway. She drops her laundry basket. I grab her arm and shove her into the room. She lands on the floor at Emerson's feet. He pulls her up off the floor. Her fingers trail along his face as if she's trying to commit his face to memory.

"Oh my God, you're alive."

"It would seem so."

"How is that possible?"

"Jake's been keeping me a prisoner here for months."

She turns and tries to bolt from the room. I block her path and with my hand around her throat, I lift her up and toss her back onto the floor.

"I'll be back tomorrow for your answer. Maybe Ro will be able to convince you how far I'm willing to go." I step back and the door closes. Picking up the laundry basket and gathering all the clothes. I bring it into the laundry room. I head back upstairs; no one is the wiser. Except now, I have the two of them to dispose of.

Roslyn

I can not believe I'm sitting here with Emerson. A very *undead* Emerson, in a room inside my own house that I never knew existed. "How are you even here? I mean alive. And who did we have a memorial for? How long has this room been here? How long have you been here?"

"You mean to tell me you knew nothing about this room?"

"No, but then again, my whole marriage has been nothing but a facade for a very long time. How are you here? You're dead. You were cremated."

"How are Bailey and the kids?"

He's got the balls to ask about his family! "How the fuck do you think they are? Their world has been turned upside down. How long have you been hidden away here?"

"Thanks to your husband, I've been here since the day I dropped dead in the court room."

"Don't you think faking your death is a little bit elaborate? I mean, if you really wanted out of your life, why not get divorced?"

"I didn't want out of my life with my family, I just wanted out of a bad situation. The dead thing was Jake's idea."

"Why?"

"He said we would be safe, and that's all that mattered to me."

I glance around the room and then back towards Emerson. "Two people have been kidnapped and there are guards all over your family. Is that what you were hoping for?"

"Of course not! I thought Jake knew what he was doing."

"Well, apparently, not since you're locked in this room. How did he do it? I mean there were cameras in that courtroom. We all saw you go down."

"In the weeks leading up to my death, Jake had me sit down with a prosthetic makeup artist that owed him a big favor. She made a replica of my face. When the time came, Jake gave me a drug to take during my closing argument. It was his crew that took me away in the ambulance. By the time we got to the hospital, there was a John Doe with my face on the gurney. I had already come to, changed my clothes and became one of the paramedics. When it was time for the next of kin notification, Bailey was brought into a sitting room where the morgue attendant showed her a photograph. That's it, that's all there is to it. Nothing like you see on television, Ro. No one is brought into the morgue where the attendant pulls back the sheet for dramatic effect. Jake set up a private viewing at the mortuary for my family. Which was only Bailey and the kids. I was quickly cremated, and then came the memorial for friends and colleagues. He played on the fact that Bailey was distraught. She trusted him. I mean why wouldn't she, he's my best friend.

When it was time to bring me here, Jake put me in a disguise, just in case you were home, and locked me in this room. The plan was to put me in a safe house and bring my family to me. Then I would turn everything I had over to Jake and he was going to work with all those other alphabet agencies to bring everyone in. After that, we would all get new identities."

"So what happened?"

"Jake happened. When he realized how much money was involved and how much power there was contained in the ledgers and videos, he got greedy and decided he wanted it all for himself. I refused to turn anything over to him. So, he's kept me locked up in here ever since. Now you're locked up here, too. This is not going to end well for either of us."

"Well, that's a no-brainer, at this point. Gail's been kidnapped. Bailey and the kids are blanketed with security. What exactly do you have that everyone wants?"

He quickly gives me all the details from the sex to the drugs.

"How did you ever get involved in all of this? I mean, for Christ's sake, you're a divorce attorney."

He walks up to the mini fridge and pulls out a couple of bottles of water, passing one to me. He takes a seat next to me. I'm having a hard time wrapping my mind around the fact that Emerson is sitting next to me and not dead.

"Look, we're probably going to die in here. You've already admitted to a whole bunch of shit that's got to be illegal. But, something is telling me there is more, more that you're hiding. Whatever you have done can't be that bad."

"I had a one-night stand with Regina. Megan is my kid."

"Holy shit, are you fucking serious?! Does Bailey know? How does Regina fit into all of this?"

"She blackmailed me into helping her set up the entire operation with her brother Mateo. Look, telling you everything is only rehashing all the bad stuff I've done in the name of protecting the ones I love. Year after year, the business we created grew. Now, it's one of the biggest Apps for sex out there. It was only supposed to be sex and let's face it—sex sells. It's not just the ledgers that are valuable, there are videos from every sex act that was ever performed. These people are very wealthy and very influential. That should have been enough, but then Mateo started using his proceeds to set up a his own drug business. He brought some bad people into the business and that's when I wanted out."

I'm trying to process everything he's telling me but it's like something out of a Clancy novel. "You're a divorce attorney, why would she blackmail you?"

"I have a background in accounting. When I decided to open up my own law practice, I supplemented my income with some really creative accounting practices for some of my more questionable clients while building up my business. I know where to hide the dirty money in plain site, and then bring it back clean."

"I saw your finances, Emerson. After you died, well, your nondeath. I helped Bailey go through all of it. You left her in a one hell of a mess. Obviously, you're not a very good accountant. Why would you do that?"

"I planned it to look like I was just another schnook, living above his means."

"So, what happened?"

"I told you; Jake happened. He got greedy and wanted it all. He wants Mateo and Regina out of the picture. He wants to take over the entire business for himself. Ro, the way he talked about all of this, you were never part of his equation."

I drop my head into my hands and finally let out the years of tears I've been holding back. The fear, the rape, the beatings, and the forced abortion. All my sorrow and guilt that is deep inside of me is rising to the top. The realization that Jake really is a monster no matter the amount of love I've showed him. He will never change.

I have no idea what time it is. There are no windows or clocks. I try to get a grip and pull myself together but I can't stop the tears. He has quietly sat next to me with a tissue box in his hand. The sobs are finally subsiding and now my body is in fight or flight mode. I wipe away the last of my tears, get up and take a look around, pacing like a caged animal.

"Ro, I've already looked for a way out or some way to get help. Oh, and he videos everything in here."

He points up to the camera. I take off my shoe and I'm about to take a swing at it but he jumps up, grabs my arm and pulls me up against him. I'm trying to push back but he leans in and whispers in my ear, "Don't. If by the grace of God he gets caught, I'm hoping someone will see the videos and know we are in here."

"The FBI was at our house this morning. They took our phones and computers."

"Shh. Don't give him any reason to erase the videos." He finally let's go and we sit back down.

"What about Gail? How does she fit into all of this?"

"I have no idea. The only thing I can figure out is Bailey must have turned to her for help."

"That makes sense. She came to me for financial help, why not ask Gail to help with this. Unfortunately, Gail is very kindhearted and that probably will get her killed, if it hasn't already." He winces at my words.

"You have to believe me, Ro, I never wanted anyone to get hurt. I just wanted a new start with my family."

"Unfortunately, life does not come with a remote control. There is no pause button or rewind."

We silently sit together, trapped inside the tiny room, trying to figure out where life went so very wrong for both of us.

CHAPTER
TWENTY-ONE

Gail

HE'S CURLED INTO A BALL. His teeth are chattering and he's moaning. I'm not sure if it's from needing more of the drug or from the beating he sustained. I try to move him, so I can get a look at his back. His body jerks and his eyes fly open.

"What are you doing?"

"I'm trying to see how bad your back is and if I can do anything to help you. You know, I am a doctor."

"Yeah, but you work on dead people and I'm not there yet. Where are we?"

"I have no clue."

He tries to get to his feet but he stumbles back to the ground. I hold up my arm showing him the huge chain that I'm handcuffed to. He looks from mine to his and back to mine. He pulls my chain closer towards him just as the door opens. In walks Mateo and his two goons.

"Are you prepared to talk?" He holds up a needle, so Fitz can see it.

"Don't give me anymore of that shit and I'll talk."

He unlaces the top of his boot and the goons run forward. He stops and holds his hands up.

"You already know I don't have a weapon because you're still alive. I'm just getting a paper from my boot."

Mateo nods his head and Fitz pulls out a piece of paper and passes it to him.

"What is this?"

"Proof I have the ledgers, Emerson's portion of the key, and the videos. Let Gail go and I'll give them to you—all of them deciphered—on a silver platter."

"No one leaves."

"Then, go fuck yourself."

"Eventually, Mr. Rodriguez, you'll be begging me, and it won't be to go fuck myself."

The two goons step in and hold Fitz up. He tries his best to fight them off but, in his condition, they quickly overpower him. Mateo gives him another shot and soon he falls on the floor and curls into a fetal position. The goons leave. Mateo is staring at me. "Gail, your face gives away so much. You wear your heart on your sleeve. When he comes to again, it will be worse. It's in his best interest that you convince him to give me my ledgers. It's the only way you will be able to protect him from the hell I'm going to put him through." He's laughing as he turns around and leaves. It's pure evil.

When the door bolts, Fitz's eyes fly open and that fear is etched upon his face, yet again. "Fitz, I'm here for you. What can I do?"

He's furiously trying to rub his hip, as if a bug or something is biting him. Finally, he pushes his pants down enough and I see the tattoo. When his hand is over it he closes his eyes and whispers.

"I love you MJ. Save me again, only you can."

He keeps repeating it over and over again until he finally falls unconscious.

MJ

Andy and I sat by that window for hours, waiting for something . . . anything, but everything is quiet. I keep checking my phone to make sure it's charged and the ringer is on loud. I even check Andy's phone since he can never remember to charge the damn thing . . . Nothing.

Andy has been in the kitchen with Patrick for awhile now. When he gets nervous, he cooks. The video monitor for the front door comes to life and my heart skips a beat. Until I see it's Travis and Livy. I buzz them in, praying they've got something—anything. Patrick hears Livy and comes running. She scoops him up and dances around the room with him. His laughter is what calms me.

"Travis, tell me you've found him, please." I'm barely able to croak out my plea.

"I'll find him, MJ. There's still too much here that is left undone. And when I find him, I'm kicking his ass. For now, I'm going to take over your dining room. I have a lot of stuff to go through. My team will also tap into yours and Andy's phones, just in case."

Within minutes, my house is filled to the max. FBI, DEA, ATF: you name it, they're here. Everyone, that is, but Fitz. I take my coffee and sit by the window, mindlessly rubbing my tat as I pray for his safe return. I continue my mantra over and over again. *He's not dead.* He can't be; my heart is still beating. *Follow my heartbeat, Fitz. Find your way back to me—to us.* Patrick comes running in, distracting me from my thoughts.

"Hey, little man." I open my arms and he leaps into them. My son is proof that life goes on, no matter what happens. Livy sits down next to me.

"He's a ball of energy."

"I'm lucky that Stella is here every day. She keeps him amused and tires him out."

"Stella is such an easy going kid. She's really adjusted well, living with Andy. I'm happy for both of them."

"Are you going to ask me? Everyone else is avoiding it. Lucas thinks I'm in shock. Andy thinks I'm in denial."

She puts her arm around my shoulder and gives it a gentle squeeze. "MJ, I know you. If you want to talk about it, you will. In your heart, you believe he's not dead. I'm going with that. I learned a long time ago to never second-guess you guys. Hell, his tenacity and your faith in him saved my life once before, so why would I ever doubt you?"

"Thank you. Do you think all these people really know what they are doing?"

"Yes, each one will fill a different piece of the puzzle."

The buzzer rings and the surveillance screen lights up; Sal's here. Travis buzzes him in and he must be taking the steps two at a time. He's a big man; I can feel the house shake. He barrels through the door half out of breath. My heart skips a beat. Maybe he found Fitz. I scoop Patrick up and take a few steps towards him. For a split second, my heart surges until he shakes his head no. My heart sinks again. My hope is reminding me not to give up. I go back to my window seat, trying to suppress my fear, waiting for my Superman. "Come home, Fitz," I whisper.

Sal hurries over to Travis. "I found the ledgers and the videos!"

All the agents gather around him. Apparently, he has what they have all been searching for. Earlier, I heard one of the agents talking and he said whomever has these ledgers is sitting on a gold mine. I've seen the best and the worst society has to offer and it usually comes down to greed. How far will someone go to possess stuff?" When is it enough? Is it ever enough? Travis and Sal are glued to the computer, everyone else is just standing around doing nothing.

"Livy, can you do me a favor and take Patrick for a minute?" Thankfully, she doesn't question me. I head into my dining room, the hub for this whole operation. I assess the room, along with the adjoining kitchen. There are men and women standing around, doing absolutely nothing, at my husband's and Gail's expense. I grab the back of the chair and steady myself. After I count to ten, I take a few deep-calming breaths, not for me, for the safety of the people around me.

"Travis, Sal, how will this help get my husband and Gail back?"

Sal stops what he's doing, looks at Travis and then back to me. Travis gets up and comes over to me. He puts his hands on my shoulders. This man has put his life on the line for me more than once. I trust him to give me the truth.

"Right now, Sal is creating a dummy file. I'm going to try and negotiate a trade: the files they want for Fitz and Gail. When this new file is opened, and the user gets to page ten, it releases a virus that I created. Not only will it corrupt their entire system, it will also automatically send me all their contacts and prior emails. I promise you, I'm doing all that I can."

"I know you are, but is it necessary to have all of these people standing here with their thumbs up their ass?" I sweep my hand across the room for emphasis. I hear Sal laugh and then he turns red when our eyes meet.

"MJ, if the shoe was on the other foot, Fitz would be doing the same thing for me. And Livy would be just as worried as you are. I'm going to find him and bring him home. I promise."

"Okay, but do something with them. They don't seem to believe you." I turn and walk out of the room. I don't want that kind of negativity around me. I go back to my window seat and wait.

CHAPTER
TWENTY-TWO

Gail

FITZ FINALLY STOPPED MOANING AND calling out for MJ. It's cold and damp. One minute he's sweating and the next, he's shivering. I know it's the drugs they are filling him with. Mateo has been coming in every couple of hours and shooting him up with more each time. I don't know how much more of this he's going to be able to take. It's only a matter of time before he OD's on this junk. I pulled the crate over, so I can have something to lean against while I have his head in my lap. I'm trying to offer him some sort of comfort.

They always say hindsight is 20/20. Who are these assholes that say that? I sat here, looking back over the last seventeen years. I thought I knew these girls. Even knowing what I know now, I never would have believed this could be true. True friends don't do this shit. Adultery, blackmail, and God knows what else. Was Bailey involved in any of this? What about Ro? How much did she know? I don't know what the truth is anymore. These girls are my family, the only family I have. I would have bet my life on these girls. Now, it looks like I just might have. I don't think I could ever trust another person ever again. That is, if I even get out of here alive. Maybe this is why I'm a loner. This is why I'm more comfortable working with the dead than the living. At least the dead don't lie.

His eyes open but then he quickly closes them to a squint. "Fitz, talk to me."

He rolls his head towards me and smiles! "What the hell are you smiling for?"

"We're in a predicament but we're still alive. Besides, I have a plan." He puts his fingers under my chin and pushes my mouth closed. "You trying to catch some flies?"

He laughs and I pull a piece of his hair. "Brat."

He tries to stretch out but winces. No doubt, it's painful.

"Gail, how are your ribs? Are they broken?"

"I don't think they are broken but, like you said, I work on dead people, so what the hell do I know?" I'm giving it right back to him and I have to say, it feels good . . . damn good.

"I'm sorry," he says. He puts his fingers under my chin and closes my mouth yet again. "Flies, Gail."

"I can't help it if you keep surprising me. Now, tell me what the hell do you have to be sorry about?"

"I didn't mean to insult you. I know you are a great doctor. Besides, I was supposed to save you, not get caught. So, I'm sorry about that, too."

I swat at the air, dismissing his hero complex like an annoying fly sticking to your face on a hot summer day. "Did you figure out what that paper was that Bailey found?"

He pulls himself up, wincing as he does, so he's now sitting across from me.

"It's all about sex and drugs. Apparently, Mateo, Regina, and Emerson each have a piece of an electronic key. When all three parts come together, they unlock an account with millions of dollars."

"But Bailey said Emerson left her in a financial mess. How is that even possible?"

He closes his eyes and begins rubbing his temples. I'm not sure how much longer he will be lucid before he begins to feel the effects of not having the drug. Or they come in and shoot him up again.

"If this is too much for you now, we can wait."

"Time is not our friend. Anyway, maybe that's what he wanted people to believe. We will never know, because he's dead. The express version is the three of them created a pay to play sex app. No sexual act was off limits, but the kinkier it got the higher the price."

"I know Emerson's letter said Regina was blackmailing him, but if you would have known him, you would be shocked to hear he was involved in all of this. He was a good guy, Fitz. He did a lot of pro bono work on cases that were considered a lost cause. I just can't understand why."

"You read the letter, Gail. He made a mistake and truth be told, I think he was set up. After that, he was protecting his family. On that note, I can understand. I would walk through fire and hell to protect my family." His words hurt. I know they are not intentional, but I got him into this situation and now he might lose it all. "Anyway, Mateo brought drugs into the equation. He needs access to the money to pay off his China connection. Without it, Mateo is a dead man."

"So the ledgers and videos that Emerson talked about in his letter documents all of this?"

"Yes, Emerson hid it and now everyone wants it. It's the holy grail of blackmail material."

"It's bizarre to think all of this was happening in our Long Island town, and for what—money? This country is in a crisis with the opioid addiction and it's people like this that are adding fuel to the fire!"

"A lot of times, it's right in our own backyard and we don't even know it."

I need to ask him what he heard. I just don't know how. I've kept my secret for so long. Mateo exposed it like ripping a band-aid off a scab.

"Gail, what's wrong? Well, I mean other than the fact that we are being held captive by a madman."

Here goes nothing. "How much did you hear Mateo say to me about you?"

I can actually see the movie reel in his head replaying everything that happened. He finally looks me in the eye and I can see when the realization hits him. His cheeks blush, something I've never seen on him.

"Oh, um, I just thought he was throwing shit out there to see what would stick."

If only that was the case. "This can of worms has been opened and I think after seventeen years, I need to tell you the truth. I owe that much to myself too." Before I continue, I move closer so I'm directly across from him.

"When I first met you, I thought you were a player. You were always playful with all the ladies. Then, when I really got to know you, I found out it was just the opposite. I found you quirky, interesting, and a loner. I wanted to get to know you more." I reach over with my fingers and lift his chin. "Now, who's trying to catch flies?"

He's staring at me like I have two heads. I continue on with my story, not waiting for a response. "I've always been a book nerd and work kept me so busy. When that nut, Mark Chambers, shot you, I realized how short life could be. I finally worked up the nerve to tell you how I felt. So, I went to the hospital that day to tell you and you had just proposed to MJ. I saw something in you that day that I never saw before. It was like you finally found peace. You'll always hold a special place in my heart, but I know it was never meant to be. Anyway, you're happy and I'm happy for you.

"The thing is, Mateo picked up on it. I'm afraid he will torture you even more because of it. Maybe even go after your family. I don't think I could live with myself if something happened to any of them."

He's very quiet, staring at me with a look I've never seen before. "Please, Fitz, don't pity me. Like I said, I'm happy for you, really I am."

"It's not pity, Gail. More like shock. I'm sorry I never picked up on it. I wish you had said something. I would have told you right off the bat not to waste your time on the likes of someone like me. You need to understand; it has nothing to do with you. I was a loner because I couldn't be with anyone. My life was a mess. I was a broken man, filled with fear and self-loathing. I know you heard me earlier begging MJ to save me again. See, she really did save me. One of the hardest things in the world to find is your purpose in life. To find the reason you exist. Some people search their whole life and never find it. Because of her, I found myself. I found my purpose in life. I stopped hating myself. I've come to accept my past and finally put it to rest. That only came when I finally let MJ in."

Maybe he's just trying to make me feel better. "You seemed pretty well put together when we met."

"I was anything but. Look at me, Gail. I can't even be in a room with the door locked. Maybe you should ask yourself how *big tough guy Fitz* can get through the toughest of days, yet, the sound of a lock makes his blood run cold. If I gave into it, the fear would cripple me."

"I saw the extreme look of fear on your face when Mateo bolted that door. I didn't understand it. Why?"

"I've looked in the eyes of death before and it's not a place I want to visit again anytime soon."

He looks down at his hands and that's when I notice they are shaking. I'm not sure if it's from the drugs or his fear. "If it's too much, you don't have to share it. I'll take your word for it."

"No, you need to hear this. Maybe then you'll understand me more. When I was a small boy, my biological father beat my mom and me. When I was six years old, my mom locked me in the bathroom to keep me safe. To keep my father from beating me to a pulp all because I left my bike outside. He beat my mother to death outside that door. I laid on the bathroom floor for three days looking at her from the space under the door. I watched him kill her and I. Did. Nothing. I watched as the life left her. Have you ever watched someone die, Gail?"

"No, I've never seen anyone die. I've worked with the families after they are dead. I try to make sense of it for them."

"Well, seeing it changes you. Anyway, after three days Andy told his dad that I never showed up to work on our project for school. As you know, he was a cop. Before he went to work, he came around the corner to check on me. That's when he found my mom. He heard me crying and realized where I was. He found the key for the padlock, came in, and saved me. He tried to shield me from looking at her but it didn't matter. I already watched her die at the hands of my father and I did nothing. He brought me to the hospital and then he had Annie come and stay with me. Once my father was arrested, Pat pulled some strings and he and Annie took me home with them. My father eventually died in a prison fight and that's when Pat and Annie adopted me. For a long time, I felt guilty about my mom's death. I think that's why I became a cop. I couldn't save her, so I wanted to save everyone else that needed saving. The logical side of my brain knows I was only six years old and there was nothing I could have done to stop it. The emotional side of my brain lays the guilt on pretty thick at times." He takes a deep breath and runs his fingers through his hair.

"Oh, Fitz, that's so sad, but you've been able to move forward with your life."

"Yes, but you need to understand why."

"Why? Why, what?"

"Why MJ. I've been in love with her since we were kids. I never thought I was good enough for her, for anyone. As kids, I wanted to be her hero, but all I ever was is broken. Do you understand, Gail? A broken hero. She gave me strength to face my demons. Her love for me made its way through all the cracks in my heart. For years, I couldn't even sleep in a bed. I would wait until everyone went to sleep and then I would take my pillow and sleep on the bathroom floor. Every night I would have horrible nightmares. In my dreams, I would be reliving the whole thing and always trying to save my mom. Unfortunately, the outcome was always the same. Maybe that's why I slept on the bathroom floor. I felt close to her. Anyway, I figured I would be up before anyone would find out, except one day I woke up and found myself covered with her Hello Kitty blanket. After that, every night I would pretend I was asleep and wait for her to come in and cover me. She never asked me why I was sleeping on the floor. Every kind thing she has ever done for me has helped make me whole.

By the time we were old enough, I pushed her away. I was so scared that if we got together and it didn't work out, I would lose the only family I ever had. I let the fear of that possible loss cripple me. All those wasted years I thought she would never want anything to do with me. I believed I was broken and not good enough for her, for anyone."

"So, what changed?"

"When I finally opened up to her, she didn't go running for the hills. She never gave up on me. She made me understand that no one is perfect. Different is good. For the first time in my life, I realized it's okay to need someone. She completes me in a way that only she can. So, you see, no matter what you would have said or done, it wouldn't have changed anything. It has nothing to do with you. It was me. Forever with her is the only thing I know. She is my destiny."

"And now because of me, you could lose it all. Now, I feel *really* shitty."

"Well, don't. I would have taken the case even if you didn't ask me to."

"Why?"

"Because at some point in life, everyone needs help. Sometimes it's just getting up enough strength to be your own hero. Bailey and those kids, they have no one to turn to for help. I might not be perfect but I will always help, that's what keeps me balanced. It's a terrible world out there. Unfortunately, you and I, we see the worst that society has to offer. I see them when they are alive and you get them when they are dead. We both have to put the puzzle pieces together to help the survivors. To help make the world a safer place. If I can do that for my children and their children, I will."

"Okay, superhero, so how about filling me in on this great plan of yours."

Before he can, the door opens and Mateo comes in. His glare sends a chill down my spine and a knot in my stomach.

"I see the two of you are getting comfortable here."

"What do you want from us?" Fitz growls out.

"Who's next on the list that would pay to get you both back, or should I try your wife?"

I feel guilty enough; I can't let this madman anywhere near MJ. "Please—"

"Gail, I've got this. Don't worry." He balls his fists and I'm not sure if it's to stop the shaking or to control his rage. "My company has what you want. You'll have to contact them and they'll make arrangements for an exchange." He rattles off a number and then tells him to talk to Travis.

Mateo is not moving. Instead, he begins to bark out orders. His men come in and pull Fitz up like Jesus, again. This time they are taking turns beating him. I'm screaming but they don't stop. One of the men shoots him up with more drugs, telling Mateo they are doubling the dose. Fitz lets out a blood-curdling scream. Finally, one of them grabs a fist full of Fitz's hair and pulls his head back.

"Say hello to the camera, Fitz."

"Like I told you before, asshole. Go. Fuck. Yourself."

Mateo stops filming and laughs as he heads out the door. The other men let go and Fitz is once again in the fetal position on the floor. I don't know how much more his body can take.

CHAPTER
TWENTY-THREE

Bailey

SAL GATHERED ALL HIS STUFF and ran out of here. Maybe he figured out how to get Gail and Fitz back safely. I pray he has and this could finally be over. I'm glad he's through with Collin. My son has been through enough. I want to get our lives back to normal but until everything is resolved, we will be under lock and key with twenty-four seven guards. Regina came by a couple of times but the guards sent her away. I let her phone calls go to voice mail. But Megan keeps calling Lilly and that is something I can't stop right now. I have no idea how I'm going to explain all of this to my children. As parents, we want to shield our children from everything bad, but we also have to teach them that not everyone in this world is good. I have to try and explain all of this while not shredding their father to pieces. Truth is, he broke me. He destroyed everything I thought to be true and replaced it with hurt, deceit, and lies. Now, I have to rise above it all, for them.

"Mom, hello, are you all right?"

I snap out of my pity party and realize Lilly is trying to talk to me about something. "Sorry kiddo, I was lost in my thoughts. What's up?"

"What's up?! Regina keeps calling my phone. She wants to talk to you but she said you wouldn't take her calls. You need to make her stop. El blocked her number for me but now she is using Megan's phone. I don't want to block my best friend's number. I've lost my father, we can't leave the house, I don't want to lose my best friend, too."

She passes me her phone but I hold my hand up. "I'll call her from my phone. I promise. I just have to make a quick call."

"Fine, let me know when it's safe to answer my phone again." She turns and leaves in a huff.

Before I call her, I've got to talk to Sal.

Me: I've been holding out talking to Regina but she is harassing Lilly. I'm going to have to call her. What do you want me to say?

Sal: She's got to know by now that you know things you probably shouldn't. Especially with all the security Fitz put around you and the kids. Have you heard from your friend Roslyn?

Me: No, which is odd. She usually checks in on me all the time. Do you think they have her too?

Sal: No. Let me talk to everyone and figure out what you should do about Regina. Sit tight. I'll call you in ten minutes.

He makes me laugh—*sit tight*; what else is there for me to do? Oh, Emerson, I could have dealt with everything you did, except sleeping with Regina. Now I'm second-guessing everything I think I should say and do. This has got to stop. I have three kids depending on me. I have no one to depend on. My phone lights up and it's Sal calling. At least *he's* keeping his word.

"Hey, what did everyone decide?"

"Don't call her. Less is always more. The less she knows the more advantage we have. I know it's not what you wanted to hear, but I promised to keep you in the loop."

"Okay, I'll talk to Lilly."

"When you're ready to talk to the kids about Megan, I can come over for moral support."

"Thank you, Sal. I just might take you up on that."

"Okay, I'll keep you posted."

He hangs up and now I need to deliver the news.

Travis

I know MJ is scared. I'm scared for him, too. I was able to trace Mateo and Regina's family back to a Colombian cartel. They've been in this country for seventeen years but they have ties with some bad people. I keep replaying the proof of life video of Gail that Hart sent me along with the video Fitz sent that Tito took. Somehow all this ties together, I just can't figure out how.

Tito was a good man who worked hard to get out of the path he was heading down. Tito stopped filming when he saw the man in the baseball cap. I'm going to start there. I pull the image out of the video and start running it through the agency's facial recognitions system. In just a few minutes I get a hit: Martinez Sanchez. The name means nothing but he has a sealed juvie record. I could lose my job for what I'm about to do or at least be reprimanded. I take a deep breath and after a few clicks, I'm in the archived juvie records. I unseal his record. It's long and he used the system like a revolving door. When he turned sixteen, his uncle vouched for him and got his juvie record sealed. He went to live with the uncle and his cousin Tito. Damn it!

"Sal, I figured out why Tito stopped filming and tried to get Hudson away from the crime scene. The man in the video is Martinez Sanchez, Tito's cousin. He probably recognized him and knew something we didn't. We need to get a warrant out for his arrest." All of the agents from the different agencies gather around my computer and I show them all the information. They begin barking out orders. Unfortunately, even if they get this guy, he's just a low-level flunky.

My phone rings with an unfamiliar number. "Hello, this is Travis."

"I believe you have something I want. I'm willing to make a trade."

"Who is this?"

"Every minute you play games with me cuts into the time they have to live. I'm sending you a video. I'll call you back in ten minutes. That should give you enough time to realize how serious this situation is."

He hangs up before I could say a word. My phone beeps, notifying me I have a video. I open it up and hit play . . . *Jesus Christ.* What the hell are they doing to him? When he let's out a blood-curdling scream, I hear a crash and MJ screaming.

"Fitz! Travis, where is he? Fitz!"

Livy and two agents are trying to hold her back. I can't let her see this. It would break her, and Fitz would kill me.

"MJ, you need to pull it together. I know this is bad, but he's alive. Any second that phone is going to ring and I'm going to have to do the best negotiation of my life to get them back. I can't do that if I'm worried about you losing it!" I know I'm harsh but I also know what I'm dealing with. She crumbles to the floor in Livy's arms. At least I know she'll be safe there. I'm waiting for the call back and I see Andy standing there. I realize he was behind me. He had to have seen the video. He says nothing, only putting his hands together, drops to his knees and begins to pray. Time ticks by very slowly. All the praying and staring at my phone is not going to make it ring.

Roslyn

"We need to figure out how to get out of here." I keep pacing around the room like some caged animal. Bad enough I've been trapped in Hell, at least, that's what my marriage has been; my space only got smaller.

"Don't you think I've tried? Ro, you're going crazy and you haven't even been here that long. I've been in here for over three months! I've tried everything I can think of."

"Isn't there some sort of failsafe switch or something in case someone gets trapped in here?"

"If there is, I couldn't find it. At least he put all the conveniences in here: television, bathroom, air conditioning, everything but a phone."

That's when it hits me—the phone! I had the small house phone, that is no bigger than a cell phone, tucked in the waistband of my yoga pants. It had to have come out when Jake threw me into the room. I get on my knees and begin feeling under the couch. I try to keep my back to the cameras. Let Jake try to figure out what I'm doing. I finally feel it and hold it tightly in my hand. I lean into Emerson and whisper, "Are there any cameras or audio in the bathroom?" Thinking about it grosses me out, but I put nothing past Jake. He shakes his head no. I get up and head in there. I look back and him and cock my head. He gets the hint and follows me in.

"What's going on?" he whispers so low, I have to strain to hear him.

"I was so overwhelmed with everything, I forgot I had my phone." I pull it out and it still has some battery life left. "Damn it! All I get is static. This won't do us any good."

I raise my arm to throw it against the wall in disgust, but he grabs my arm, stopping me. He takes the phone from my hand. "Go outside the bathroom or he might get suspicious." As he pushes me out the door he whispers in my ear, "Don't look at me; pretend you're doing something."

I know he doesn't want Jake to know I still have my house phone, but it's no good, so who cares?

"What are you going to do? I told you it's not working right. This basement has always had terrible service if the phone is not near the base."

"I read that all phones are required to support *911* services. They might not be able to use their GPS system to find us, but we can tell them where we are."

"They won't believe you, you're supposed to be dead. Try explaining that one."

"Then you call."

He dials *911* and it connects! He pulls me into the bathroom and quickly passes the phone to me.

"*911* how can I help you?"

"I don't have a lot of time. My husband has locked my friend and I in a panic room that is hidden in the basement of my home. My husband is Jake Daniels, and I think he wants to kill me."

I rattle off the address and then I hear the operator.

"I'm dispatching emergency service now. Are you in a safe area?"

Is she serious? "I'm locked inside a panic room. Once my

husband realizes I've called you, it will not be a safe place. He is a prosecutor in Manhattan. Please don't let the police leave without getting us out of here. I fear for our lives"

"What's your name?"

"Roslyn Daniels."

She tells me that she'll stay on the phone with me but the call drops and the battery is now totally dead.

"Emerson, the call is gone."

He takes the phone and keeps trying—nothing. He presses his ear to the door but I'm sure this room is probably sound proof. So much time has passed. If they were going to rescue us, they would have been here by now.

"I don't think anyone is coming to get us."

The door to the panic room begins to slowly slide open. Emerson steps away from the door. Just when I think my luck has changed, standing in the doorway is Jake, alone. How is this even possible? He points his gun at me. Jake puts his hand out and Emerson puts the phone in it.

"Thank you. I assured the officers that I will find out who made the call and make sure she understands the ramifications of her actions. They bought it, especially when they couldn't find this room. Now, as far as the ramifications." He raises his gun, aims it at me and pulls the trigger. The force pushes me backwards and I crumble to the floor.

"Why? I put up with you for all these years, and this is how it ends? Did I ever mean anything to you?"

"No, you were a means to an end." He points the gun at Emerson and the color drains from his face. "Pull any other shit and you'll be next." He turns and leaves, and I'm left to die.

CHAPTER
TWENTY-FOUR

Hudson

W HEN YOU'RE WAITING FOR NEWS, time seems to move slower. Then again, I've never been good at waiting. Annie goes to church everyday and when she didn't show up, Father O'Neil came by to check on her. I admire someone who can have such a strong belief in the unknown. Until I met Fitz, my life was filled with lies and deceit. I think that's why I demand truth and honesty from everyone around me. Probably why I fit in so well with this family. More to the point, why they took me in and offered me hope and shelter, no questions asked. If Fitz is truly lost, it will cause a blow to this family and I don't think they will ever survive it.

Sal called a little while ago and said that they got a video. Fitz is still alive. He didn't offer up much more then that, which is not a good sign. He said he found the ledgers and figured out how to decipher them. At least now we have something to bargain with. He seemed distant, but maybe it's because of the stress he is under—hell—we're all under. He did tell me that Travis figured out Tito's video. I was shocked that it was his cousin in the crowd. Probably not as shocked as Tito. Once he realized it was him, he couldn't get us out of there fast enough. Unfortunately, he was distracted and it cost him his life.

Pat has parked himself by the front window. He hasn't moved or said a word to any of us. I've made sure he's at least drinking water. Annie has her rosary beads and she has not stopped praying since he was taken. Livy came by earlier and dropped off Patrick. Stella is always so excited to see him. To her, he's a real live doll. They are a good distraction, but Fitz is never far from my thoughts.

Sal

My call to Hudson was strained. She knows something's off but for whatever reason she hasn't questioned me about it, at least not yet. I put on my headset, so I can replay the video without upsetting MJ or Andy. There has to be some sort of clue I can pull from it. Suddenly, I realize I never saw the first video with just Gail. "Travis, I need a copy of the first video with just Gail."

"Sure. What are you thinking?"

"I never saw it. I'm thinking maybe with fresh eyes, and if I play them side by side, I can get something from the location."

He air drops it from his laptop to mine and I first run it as it was sent. I'm sure when Fitz saw Mateo kick Gail, it sent him into high gear. I have all kinds of programs that I've designed that can manipulate any kind of video. Maybe if I take out the voices, I can pick up something in the background.

Nothing, damn it! I feel a headache coming on. I get up to stretch my legs and head into the kitchen for some coffee. I find a very animated Travis on the phone. I'm praying that maybe we've caught a break.

"Sal, that was Hart. Apparently a *911* call came in from Jake's house. The call was from a woman claiming to be his wife. She said she was being held against her will along with her friend in a panic room in the basement. The police were dispatched and Jake claimed a neighbor kid pulled a prank. The police looked around and found nothing. We were there earlier and we didn't find anything. I'm sending the call to your phone. I have a crew ready to go with you. The caller said there is a hidden room in the basement, but the officers didn't find anything. I want you to tear that place apart. I don't care if you have to rip the walls down!"

Even with lights and sirens, it takes us twenty minutes to get to Jake's house. The recording from *911* had a lot of static. I cleaned it up the best I could. The woman identified herself as his wife.

He was not too happy to let us in again, but after I toss the warrant at his feet he realized he had no choice and stepped aside. The men begin the search while I watch Jake. It reminds me of a game I used to play with my baby sister. I would hide something of hers and she would have to find it. Every time she got closer to it I would say "You're getting warmer" until she was on top of it and then I would tell her she was burning up. Eventually, she would find it. It always took her so long, though. She would get mad at me cuz I would find whatever she hid so quickly. It was her facial expressions that gave it away. This is no different from that game.

We head downstairs, Jake watching my every move. The men are tapping on the walls and the floors, trying to see if there is a difference in the sound. Not me, I'm watching Jake's face. I walk towards the TV and his eyes narrow. That's when I notice the TV is not plugged in. Why have a stadium size television and not plug it in? I take a step closer towards it but I'm watching his face the whole time. He's starting to sweat and I know I'm on to something. I look down and notice two remotes and only one television. His eyes glance at the remotes and then he takes a small step backwards. That's it, he blinked first. I pull my gun and aim it at his head. Every agent in the room stops, their hand on their weapon, ready to assist. Jake puts both his hands up.

"Now, why don't you tell me where the panic room is."

"I think you've lost your mind. I've cooperated with you and yet you've got a gun pointed at me."

"Which remote is it?"

And there it is, the realization that I've got him and there is no getting out of here.

"I want a deal."

I take a step closer. I'm a very big guy and with my gun in hand, I'm coming right at him. "Which remote?"

"The shorter one. Give me a deal and I'll give you the code to open it. Without that they will eventually run out of air. Their death will be on you."

He said *they* will run out of air. One of the agents comes behind him and cuffs him. Double-checking him again for weapons.

"What's the code?" Now he has the balls to have a cocky ass smirk on his face.

"Let them fucking die. I don't get a deal, I don't talk."

I turn to the agents standing next to him. "Hold him." They take hold of him for me.

"You don't scare me; you're a cop. Nothing but a flunky, following the rules."

"You see, Jake, that's where you're wrong. I'm not a cop, asshole. You see all of these men and women know Fitz and they know what's at stake here. Do you think anyone of them will help you?"

I step closer and yank down his sweats. I point my Glock an

inch from his sorry little cock. "Just as I figured, not much there, bucky. So, here is your deal. You tell me the code and you get to keep your sorry excuse for a dick. Don't tell me the code and I shoot it right off of you. If that happens, you will spend your life in prison quite literally as someone's bitch." The sweat is running down his face and I can't help but smile. That's when he turns as white a snow. Guess he realizes I'm serious.

"Okay, deal. It's the wall behind you. The code is 3825 now please pick my pants up."

When I punch in the code the wall slides open. Behind the wall is a dead woman who I'm assuming is Roslyn Daniels and a very undead Emerson Davis.

Travis

The call from Sal damn near made me lose my shit. My best friend is in a fight for his life right now. And all this time, Emerson has been alive. He had Jake help him fake his own death and then chickened out of the follow through! He better hope I find Fitz alive or I'll rip him apart with my bare hands.

I keep playing both proof of life videos. Something is there, but I can't pull it from the back of my brain. Livy walks in the room and massages my temples, trying to ward off the migraine I feel coming on.

"What can I do to help?"

"I know there is a clue somewhere in all of this, but I can't figure it out."

"Get up; let me have a go at it."

What the hell, it can't hurt. I watch the screen as she runs it through a program she helped create that takes people out of videos and stills. Like they were never there. Then it enhances all the objects in the room. That's when it hits me. "The crate—goddamn it—the crate! Look at the name on the side. Blow the damn thing up, Livy."

I'm watching as she cleans it up and brings the name to life. It could be something or it could be nothing. It has the name of a chemical factory on the side of it. A quick Google search and the company was located in Queens. They are no longer in business and the building is abandoned. There is a list of these abandoned buildings and people come from all over to tour them. This one is listed as one of the top ten creepiest buildings. Apparently, the number one building was an old insane asylum. Why? People need to get a fucking life.

I gather everyone and let them know where we are going. It's a huge building and I want to make sure I have enough manpower. Livy calls Hart to let him know where we're headed. He's sending extra bodies to help us. He's going to the station to interrogate Emerson and Jake, just in case we are wrong about the location. As we head out, MJ and Andy are waiting for us.

"You're not going without us, so don't even attempt it."

"I wouldn't dream of it, but please stay in the car. If something happened to either of you, I could never live with myself."

We head out and I'm hoping it's not too late.

CHAPTER
TWENTY-FIVE

Mateo

Regina: Can you talk?

Me: Can't it wait?

Regina: No.

My phone rings before she even gives me a chance to respond to her text. "This better be important. I delivered the latest video and I was getting ready to call the guy to make the trade."

"I guess you haven't seen the news."

"Do you think I'm sitting around with nothing else better to do than to watch TV?"

"Yeah, well maybe you should. It's all over the news; Ro is dead, and Emerson is alive. And to top that off, Ro's husband, Jake, was arrested"

"Excuse me? Did you just say Emerson is alive? Then who the fuck did they bury? Who killed Ro? Why did they arrest Jake?"

Not that I cared about Ro but she wasn't even mixed up in any of this, at least, I didn't think so.

"Jake shot her. He was holding Emerson hostage until he got his hands on everything. I've got a friend in Jake's office, and she said the shit is about to hit the fan. I'm not waiting around to find out if any of it is true. I'm getting the hell out of here and I think you should, too. There is no way you're getting your hands on anything. Cut your losses and get out."

She has no clue how dangerous my China connection is. I've conveniently left that part out when I got everyone involved.

"Where are you going?"

"Home, to Colombia, Mateo, and you should go, too. Uncle Santillana will protect us."

"What about Megan?"

"I never wanted her to begin with, why would I take her with me? I have to protect myself, and you should do the same." The call ends and I realize she just hung up on me. No goodbye, nothing. It's every man for himself.

Gail

He's wet and cold. He's shivering so bad that I'm afraid of him getting hypothermia, but I really have nothing to help warm him up. He smiles as I try to keep rubbing his massive arms to warm him up. "You're coming to again and you're smiling . . . amazing."

"Not really. I'm thinking about my family. Now *they* are amazing. They will make sure we are found."

I need to keep him talking and lucid. It doesn't matter if it's mindless stuff, as long as he stays awake.

"Did you ever think it would be as easy as you make it seem to stay with one person forever?"

"For me, it is easy. It's not just about saying the words, Gail. I find a million different ways to show her I love her. Over time, love evolves and changes. Those changes are good because our roots are strong. It's like a tree. When you first plant the tree, the limbs are young and they bend. As the tree grows, the roots take and they burrow deep. When the storm comes, the tree will bend but it will always come back and stand up straight. Like I said . . . easy."

"What if there is a tornado or a hurricane?" Now I'm just messing with him. He knows it and laughs.

"Oh, Gail, after all these years, you know I don't subscribe to what if's."

I wave my hand and I'm reminded that I'm still cuffed to a chain. "Now that you're lucid, maybe we can discuss your escape plan."

"I'm going to unlock your cuffs. Just past that table, where Mateo has the drugs, there is a window. You are going to go out that window and run like the devil is crawling up your ass. Don't look back and don't worry about me. I'm sure Travis is working the first video Mateo took of you and the latest one of me. He'll figure out where we are but, just in case he can't, you run away from here as fast as you can. You have to promise me you'll make it, Gail." He sits up and lifts my chin again with his finger. "Flies, Gail."

"How are you going to get these cuffs off of me? It's not like we have a key." I'm holding them up as if he needs reminding that we are locked up.

"I need access to your bra."

"Excuse me?!" I nearly choke on my own words.

"I would have you take it off but your cuffs are in the way. Just lift your shirt up so I can get at the damn thing before someone comes back!"

"Fine! Just make it fast."

In a huff I lift my shirt and he buries his face between my breasts. I'm holding my breath, not really sure what he's doing. I feel his hot breath on my chest and I think I might die from embarrassment.

My face flushes first, followed by my whole body. He's got to feel the heat that's coming off of me. If he notices, I can only hope he'll be a gentleman about it. Maybe it will help warm him up. I can finally feel what he's doing. He's using his teeth to make a hole where the underwire is. When it's big enough, he sticks his hand into my bra and pulls out the wire.

"Thanks, you can pull your shirt down now. Sorry if I embarrassed you."

I nod not knowing what to say in such an awkward situation. He takes the plastic tip off and begins working it like a key into the keyhole.

"Where the hell did you learn to do that? I know it's not part of officer training."

"I saw it on a television show. I thought it was crazy until I tested it out on MJ."

"So, this is what you do for entertainment at night with your wife."

He's smirking and I can't help but laugh. That typical Fitz light-up-the-room kind of smile.

"Pay attention now. As soon as I get this other one off, you run. Remember, no matter what happens, don't stop and don't look back. I'll be right behind you. Got it?"

"Wouldn't it be better if we went together?"

"No. Got it open. You're free. Now run!"

I give him one last hug, stumble to my feet, and take off. When I get closer to the window, it's higher then it looked. I'm in luck, next to the table is another crate. I pull it over towards the window and step up. It gives me just enough leverage to open the window. As I start to climb out, I hear Mateo and his goons come running towards me. It's two stories up. I climb on to the ledge and grab the drainpipe. The last thing I hear is Fitz yelling for me to jump. The pipe snaps and falls to the ground, taking me along with it.

Fitz

I watched Gail take that leap of faith out the window. If this is the end for me, at least I know I gave her that last chance to find true love. Mateo's goons try to grab me but I have one arm free from the handcuffs. I'm not about to make it easy for them. I'm sore and in a lot of pain but I fight with everything I have. Until I'm hit with that fucking Taser, again.

Mateo is standing over me with the needle, laughing. He has his goons hold me while he gets my arm ready to stick it in. I don't think my body can take another dose of this junk. Please, God, help me. That's when we hear sirens. He drops the needle and takes a step back. His goons are already heading out the door.

"Don't get too excited, Fitz. It's better off this way. I want you wide awake for this one."

He pulls a remote from his pocket and begins to laugh as he heads out the door.

Gail

My ribs hurt and I know I'm banged up but I take off running as best I can. I don't look back. My lungs are burning. I run through the empty lot, towards the chain link fence. I have no idea where I am or where I'm going. But I run in a straight line. All I know is that fence means freedom. I take note what's on the other side of the fence. In the distance, there is a tower that runs a straight line to the window I jumped out of. I'm running towards the setting sun, *so that's west.* There is no way I'll be able to climb the fence, not with my ribs the way they are. I grab ahold anyway because I know it's my only way out. It's what he would want me to do—survive.

I promised him I wouldn't look back. But I can hear a car and it's getting louder. No, no, no. I'm about to try to climb the fence when I hear police sirens. Then I feel the ground begin to shake. I give up and look back over my shoulder hoping the police are coming to save us. The building is imploding. A huge cloud of dust is headed towards me. I drop to my knees, take a deep breath, pinch my nose and close my eyes. I can feel it when the dust rolls over me. I'm being pelted with all kinds of debris. The noise is so loud, it sounds like a freight train is headed my way. I can't hold my breath any longer. I try to take short, shallow breaths. When the noise finally stops, I open my eyes. There are at least a dozens cop cars surrounding a car. The doors open and out steps Mateo and his two goons with their hands up—no Fitz. He never made it out. He's always a hero for everyone else but himself.

In the distance I see MJ and Andy jump out of a car and try to run towards the building but officers are holding them back. The ringing in my ears is so loud I can't make out anything anyone is saying. The EMT's come running and begin working on me. I need to tell Travis where I last saw Fitz. They're trying to load me into an ambulance.

"I CAN'T LEAVE YET. PLEASE LET ME GO!" I can't hear but I must have yelled cause the EMT just jumped back so far, he nearly fell out. I'm kicking and screaming. They are not listening to me. I begin to yell Travis's name over and over again, as loud as I can. Finally, he steps into view.

"TRAVIS! I CAME OUT OF THE WEST SIDE OF THE

BUILDING ON THE SECOND FLOOR. HE WAS SUPPOSED TO BE BEHIND ME, JUST AS SOON AS HE GOT HIS CUFFS OFF. FIND HIM, TRAVIS, PLEASE!"

He jumps out of the ambulance and takes off running. The ambulance doors close and they take off.

"I'm so sorry, MJ. So very, very sorry."

FITZ

I feel the weight on me crushing my chest, making it hard to breathe. I thought I saw charges set up around the perimeter of the room, but then I thought the drugs were messing with my mind. I think I'm still alive. I hold up my hand with the cuff still on it. Yep, still alive. Still in a big mess and I lost the bra wire. I begin to laugh and I can't stop. I could just picture Gail trying to explain the bra thing. Five bucks says she'll be as red as a beet.

I don't know how much air I'll have. I try to move but I'm pinned under a whole bunch of rubble. Logically, when the building went down, my floor should have collapsed down to the basement. Then again, I'm just guessing. It's not like I hang out in collapsing buildings every day.

I'm so thirsty. Dehydration will probably kill me before anything else. If Gail is safe, then she can tell them where I am. I'm so tired. I have to close my eyes. I need to conserve my air and my strength. Just a few minutes, God; wake me when they get here.

CHAPTER
TWENTY-SIX

Travis

WHEN GAIL SAID HE WAS still in there, I did what any best friend would do: I ran to try and save him. The dust has finally settled and I'm standing in front of a pile of rubble. There is no building left. I've never felt this hopeless. He always has a plan and when he didn't, he flew by the seat of his pants. Now he's relying on me to come up with a plan and I don't know that I have it in me.

Sal runs up and stops dead when he sees what's left of the building. "My, God, he's in there?"

"That's what Gail said. She went out the window on the second floor. She said the west side of the building."

"He could be in an air pocket or survival pocket."

I pry my eyes away from the building and grab Sal's shoulders. "What do you know about rescuing someone from a collapsed building?"

"My dad died on *9/11*.When the planes hit, he ran into the

North Tower to help get people out. He didn't make it out. After that, I researched everything I could about how to rescue people from a collapsed building. I also took every class available, so that if ever I was given the chance, I could help save lives."

"I'm going to need you to head this up. Can you do that?"

"You don't have to ask; it's Fitz, we will all do whatever necessary to save him."

I take a deep, steadying breath. "You believe he could still be alive?"

He laughs. Not quite what I was expecting.

"Travis, it's Fitz. That man defies all logic. Now, let's get started."

He takes my radio and begins barking out orders. Everything from listening equipment to dog teams. I'm watching him work and for the first time today, I actually have hope. I have to talk to MJ and Andy. I need to let them know what's going on. I jog back towards the barricade where I know they'll be waiting. What I find stops me in my tracks. There is a sea of blue. Cops from all different houses have showed up to help search. Fitz's parents are passing out bottled water. Hudson is giving out masks and hardhats. While Father O'Neil offers prayers and hope.

I pull MJ and Andy aside. "Where are the kids?"

"Livy is watching them. She knew this is where we needed to be. Travis, you can't hold me back here. I need to find my husband."

"I would normally tell the family to go home and wait, but I know you'll turn a deaf ear. Give me a minute to give some directions to everyone and then we can get started."

The dogs have arrived, along with the listening equipment. Trucks are pulling up with heavy equipment. Time is not our friend. We quickly get organized and then start our search.

FITZ

"Fitz, wake up. How do you expect to be found if you're sleeping?"

My eyes fly open at the sound of a voice. I quickly look around but I'm alone and still in a bad situation. "What the hell? Now I'm hearing voices and talking to myself."

If Gail made it, then people will be looking for me. I need to make noise, otherwise, how will they find me? I'm pinned and no matter how much I try to move, I can't. I'm finding it hard to breathe. Damn it, my family needs me. "Come on, God, help a former alter boy out here."

"Why?"

"What the . . ." I know I talk to God. Isn't that part of what we are doing at church? When things in my life get crazy or bad, I turn to my faith. I ask God for help or guidance. But I've never had him talk back to me. Maybe it's the drugs. I only guessed what Mateo was putting in that needle but God only knows what it really was.

"Yes."

"God, you need to stop doing that. Eavesdropping is not polite." *You're losing it, Fitz.* I close my eyes and try to get a grip on my situation. I'm so thirsty and all my joints hurt like a bad case of the flu. My head is starting to hurt bad. "Just in case you're wondering, God, I'm going to close my eyes for a bit." I wait. Nothing. Okay, maybe the craziness has passed.

Emerson

This is a big mess. A mess that has, most likely, cost me my family. I've been in these interrogation rooms before but never as the perp. The door opens. A man walks in and introduces himself as Captain Hart.

"You're not new to all of this, and you have been Mirandized. Do you want to talk to me?"

"I want a lawyer."

"The choice is yours. However, I think you should know that I have your wife in the next room. At this point, I'm not sure how much she was aware of. I can only assume she was a partner to all of this. Child Protective Services has been called in to take your children. I also have Jake Daniels in a room with the FBI. Oh and let's not forget Mateo and Regina. Right now they are with DEA agents. Frankly, I would rather throw the book at the whole lot of you, but right now, two of my friends are in danger. That trumps all of you. So, talk to me and give me what I need, and I might put in a good word. The choice is yours."

He gets up and is half way out the door. "Wait," I say. He turns and looks over his shoulder at me, eyes glaring. "What if I give you the ledgers and the key to all the money? Will you leave my wife and kids out of it? They knew nothing!"

"Day late and a dollar short, asshole. I've got the ledgers and they are deciphered. The money has been frozen, so no one can get their greedy hands on it. Oh, and you want me to leave your family out of it? You should have thought about that when you involved innocent people in your disgusting get-rich plan."

I'm confused. He has everything. "What else can I give you?"

"Jake on a silver platter. Along with Mateo and Regina's family in Colombia and Mateo's connection in China. I want everyone to pay dearly for what has been done to my friends, and to all the families you help ruin with that poison you're putting out on the street."

He walks out, slamming the door behind him.

FITZ

"God, are you still here?" It's eerily quiet. Just proves I was delirious. Probably from the drugs.

"Were you expecting someone else? You know I'm here all the time."

"Oh, geez, I was hoping I was slightly losing my mind."

I try to move out from under the debris. The couple of inches helps but, at this rate, I'll probably run out of air or die from hypothermia.

"Hey, God, since you're planning on hanging out with me, maybe I can ask you some questions." No answer. He doesn't seem very cooperative. I keep wiggling, at least that will keep my blood flowing.

"It depends on the questions."

"I thought maybe you left me."

"You know I'm always with you. I'm just a little busy at the moment."

Hmm I better choose wisely. "Am I dense? I mean, MJ thinks I can be when it comes to relationships and stuff. She says I'm a black and white person. I only take what people offer. I mean, look at Gail. I don't have to tell you what happened because, like you said, you're always there. Why didn't I see that she was interested in me? I mean we've been friends for seventeen years! I would have set her straight a long time ago. I feel like she might have missed out on so much because of me."

"You were in a bad place. Having a relationship with her at that point in your life would have hurt her more than your cluelessness at the time."

"Was I a bad person to her?"

"Of course not. You were a good person in a bad situation . . . kind of like right now."

Of course my God would have to have a sense of humor.

"You know, telling her what happened to me was so hard. I've finally gotten to a point where I can live with it. But telling her was like ripping off a scab." I need to ask the hard questions, the ones that made me who I am today. Okay, here goes nothing. "God, why did my mom have to die like she did?"

"I was waiting to see how long it would take you to ask me the questions that are the most difficult for you. I needed my angel to come home."

"Why did I have to see it? Why did I have to hear it? Her screams haunt me to this day." My body begins to shake, and the sweat is uncontrollable.

"I didn't choose that. I chose to end her pain and bring her home."

"God, I have to confess, it took me a long time to stop hating you for that." I close my eyes and try to will the memories from my head, from my heart. All these years and yet when I close my eyes, I'm six years old, lying on the bathroom floor, watching my mom die.

"I know, but it sent you down a path that you might not have chosen for yourself."

"You could have just told me to become a cop."

"Ask yourself this, would you have listened? If your life was different, would you be as good at what you do? Think about all the people you've saved. Where would they be today? Where would Makenna be?"

"I love MJ more than life itself. I'm sure we would have figured it out."

"How sure are you?"

"She gave my heart a home. I have faith that we both would have found the courage to trust what our hearts already knew. You taught us that."

I think I hear laughing. "God, are you laughing at me?"

"No, but like Makenna said '*dense*.'"

Who am I to argue with the man upstairs. "Let me ask you something else. What about Gail? Is she supposed to be alone her whole life? If that's the case, that's pretty sad."

"Maybe Gail needed this for closure. Maybe this will be the catalyst that will force her to open her eyes to what's been right in front of her the whole time."

"Really? Who?"

"Get some rest, you're going to need it."

"Wait! Hello, God, don't leave me with a cliff hanger!" Nothing. . .

I pull up to the hospital to see Gail. Hopefully I didn't miss her. I flash my badge and the nurse let's me know she's still in the ER. It doesn't take me long to find her; I can hear her in a heated argument. They say doctors make the worst patients and she just confirmed it.

"Why are you giving these nice people a hard time?"

"Oh, Jack, thank God you're here. Please tell them I'm fine, so I can get out of here."

I look to the doctor for some sort of guidance. He throws his hands up and rolls his eyes. That doesn't seem encouraging.

"She needs to rest. She jumped out of a two-story window. She has bruised ribs, not to mention all of the cuts and bruises. Her hearing is coming back but she still has ringing in her ears. Does that sound like someone who is good to go?"

I pull the doctor outside the curtain while the nurse can try to stop Gail from getting dressed. "Look, you know and I know that doctors are the worst at taking care of themselves. Let me take her home and I'll look after her. If you try to keep her here, she will make your life miserable."

"I'll agree to it as long as you guarantee she will not end up back in my ER. I really don't want to treat her again."

Wow she must have really pissed on his parade. "Yes, I can guarantee she won't be back here."

He signs her release papers and while she gets dressed, I get the car. It doesn't take long before she is discharged and we're on the way to her house.

"Where are you taking me? I need to get to the site to help find Fitz!"

"No, Gail, you are going home. I sprung you from that place, but you need to follow the doctor's orders. Besides, there are literally hundreds of people working on finding him."

"Shouldn't you be working this case?"

"The FBI has officially pulled me off of the case. Apparently, I can't be objective. And you know what, they're right. My best friend is buried under tons of rubble. I'm told the chances of him coming out are slim to none. However, it's Fitz and until I see for myself that he's really gone, I won't give up hope and neither should you."

She is quiet for the rest of the ride. We finally pull up into the driveway and when I look over at her, she's crying. "Hey, what's wrong?"

"My keys were in my pocketbook. I have no way to get into my own damn house."

I reach over and wipe away her tears. I press a set of keys into her hand. "While I was waiting for the call back from Mateo, I had all your locks changed. No more tears, please. I also replaced your cell phone for you. Let's get inside. I have a lot of questions."

While she gets cleaned up, I muddle my way around her gourmet kitchen. I find a can of soup along with some saltines in the closet and put everything on a tray. Not bad for a guy who knows nothing about cooking.

"I'm going to have to ask you questions. First, I want you to eat and take your ibuprofen while I get a fire going."

"Thank you, Jack, you don't have to do all of this." She's agreeable for a change.

"Nonsense, now let me ask you to walk me through everything that happened. Leave nothing out, no matter how insignificant you might think it is."

She closes her eyes and begins to retell everything that happened from the night Bailey told her about the paper till she ended up in the hospital today.

"Well, there have been some developments you're unaware of. First of all, Emerson is alive." I wait, giving her time to absorb that bombshell before I drop the next one.

"How could that be? Who did we cremate?"

"A John Doe. Jake Daniels arranged the entire thing. However his plan went south when Emerson changed his mind. I'm afraid your friend, Roslyn Daniels, lost her life. Jake shot her. He needed to make an example out of her, so Emerson would know he was serious."

The normally reserved lady I've come to care a lot about is no longer here. She finally let's go of everything she's been holding inside. I wrap my arms around her and let her cry for as long as she needs to.

CHAPTER
TWENTY-SEVEN

MJ

THERE IS A MASSIVE AMOUNT of people here. At one time or another, every one of them needed help or some sort of support. Now, when Fitz needs it the most, they are all here, ready to help him. If only it was that easy. We all wanted to run in and start digging him out, but that could have made the situation worse, as if that's even possible. I've made my way to Nathan, the man Sal appointed to run point on the recovery. He has kindly kept me in the loop. They are doing a six-sided approach to the entire area. As far as they know, the only person inside the building was Fitz. They have cut off all utilities and labeled it a *pancake collapse void*. It's exactly as it sounds. The floors have stacked on top of each other, kind of like a giant Jenga game. They are considering it a rescue until they determine that they need to switch to a recovery. My legs shake when he says recovery. No matter how much Travis tries to keep me away from hearing all of this, I make it my business to hear every word that is being said. Sal comes up next to me and takes my hand.

"MJ, you and I know this is a rescue. We are going to be on teams. You and Andy will be on mine. The first thing we will do is called *Round-the-clock*. We will get into a position around the site and shut everything off. Once we have total silence, we can listen for any tapping or noises."

"What if that doesn't work?"

"We have other options from an electronic search to a canine search. Let's take one thing at a time. Now, let's get into place."

I follow him closer to what's left of the building, and when I see the area they think Fitz is buried in, I can't help but cry out. My legs begin to sway and Andy puts his arm around me for support. I take a deep breath and begin the ring of silence, straining to hear his beautiful voice . . . *nothing*.

The longest few minutes of my life ends with all the rescuers coming back on their radio's confirming nothing.

Lucas comes running towards us with at least a dozen handlers and their dogs. "MJ, did you bring something of Fitz's?"

I pull a zip lock from my pocket. "It's one of his favorite Superman t-shirts. I took it from the hamper, so it has his scent on it."

He takes it and quickly passes it to the handlers. They spread out and begin to do the job. All we can do is watch.

Hart

When she had no more tears left, she gave in to sleep. I won't leave her alone and if I have anything to say about it, won't take her back to the site. I've spent the last few hours on the internet trying to figure out the repercussions from Fentanyl. Unfortunately, this is not the first time I have to deal with this. The problem is, I don't know if that's exactly what Mateo gave him or if he cut it with something. Every time I try to get any information, I'm given the runaround. I finally get in touch with Simmons. He's a fed that worked with us on Stella's case. He's probably one of the few feds that Fitz hasn't pissed off. I brought him up to speed and he's going to try to find out. Since I became Captain, waiting seems to be all I do. That and bark out orders.

She's starting to stir. I stoke the fire and get the ice pack ready for her, along with her ibuprofen. She tries to stretch but let's out a small yelp and stops.

"Yeah, you won't be doing any of that for awhile." I put everything down on the coffee table and head to the kitchen to make tea.

"Have you heard anything yet?"

"No. I told you I would wake you. I'm a man of my word." I don't know why I felt the need to add that. I've always assumed she had been hurt by someone and closed down. Then one day, I saw her face when Fitz entered the station. I knew she wanted something with him but I also knew the man and that nothing would ever happen. I didn't realize the depth of her feelings for him. Sadly time stands still for no one and now she's alone.

"Jack, how about I help you with the tea?"

"I know I'm clueless in the kitchen."

"Everyone has a special talent, maybe you're just saving yours for another time." She tries to laugh, holds her ribs and thinks better of it.

"Gail, I never did ask you, how did Fitz get the cuffs off of you?"

Her face turns fire engine red and now my interest is really peaked. "He used his teeth to make a hole in my bra where the wire sits. He pulled it out and was able to use it as a key."

I can't help but laugh. "I know it's not funny, but you have to admit—that is so Fitz."

"What's crazier is that he said he practiced it on MJ."

"On an off chance, did Mateo say what he was injecting Fitz with?"

"No, Fitz assumed it was the Fentanyl cut with heroin that Mateo was selling. But it could have been anything. I know I've been getting a lot of overdoses on my table from that crap. I should have grabbed the vile off of the table before I climbed out the window. All I could think of was to follow his orders and get help."

"Don't beat yourself up over it. You were following orders."

"I know, but I still feel like crap. You knit your brows together when you're worried. I'm worried too. If it was just Fentanyl the proper way to come off of it is a taper down. If they don't find him soon he'll be going through the worst kind of withdrawal, cold turkey. When Mateo's goons brought him in, they had already given him a dose. After that, they kept coming in and giving him higher dosages of that garbage. I have no idea if they gave him any more after I escaped. Mateo taunted me that he was going to keep increasing the amount to get Fitz so hooked that he would be begging him for more. He was in bad shape, Jack. They whipped him, beat him, and on top of that, the drugs." Her voice tapers off and her bottom lip begins to tremble.

"Jesus, besides being buried under all that rubble, his body is probably going through hell right now. What happens to his body during cold turkey?" My stomach is in knots. Part of me wants to know but part of me doesn't. I know what I went through with my sister, but I don't know if this is the same.

"Mild symptoms similar to the flu will begin anywhere from twelve to thirty hours after his last dose. The worst symptoms are usually on days three through five. But we need to know if it was cut with anything. That is a game changer."

"I'm waiting on a call back. I just wanted to prepare myself for what to expect if we don't find him in time, and he goes cold turkey."

"Jack, I feel so guilty. I mean, I brought him into this mess."

"Stop, we both know Fitz doesn't do anything he doesn't want to do. He knew Bailey and the kids needed help. Unfortunately, things don't always go the way we plan. C'mon, it's time to ice your ribs." I don't need her going into a pity party. She needs to remain strong; this is far from over.

She curls up on the couch with her tea and presses the ice pack to her ribs. I'm trying to keep the fire going so she doesn't feel chilled. "Jack, I want to see Bailey. Can you make it happen?"

I knew this was coming, I just didn't think it would be this soon. "She is being held as a possible accomplice. Her kids are with CPS. You're not going to be able to see her for awhile."

"I want to go to the site. Maybe I can help. I'll get dressed. Oh, and, Jack, it's not open for negotiation." She heads down the hall, and I'm left there with cold tea.

"Stubborn woman."

Fitz

It's so cold and, yet, I'm beginning to sweat. I need MJ and Patrick—they ground me. And Stella; that little girl has us all wrapped around her little finger. It has absolutely nothing to do with her being deaf. MJ and I both want more children, but nothing is happening and it's not for lack of trying. I'd ask God but I can't talk to him about that. I'll just leave that up to MJ. I'm usually so sharp with my thoughts but I'm feeling scattered. I've got to try harder to get out of here before I completely lose what's left of my mind. I wiggle enough and now I've got both hands free. Not sure what that's going to accomplish.

I hold my hands up but my right wrist still has the cuff on. You would think the heavy chain that's attached to it would have broken off when the building collapsed. No such luck. I need to make some noise, but I'm so thirsty I can hardly swallow let alone yell. Maybe I can push some of this shit off of my chest. That might make it easier to breathe.

"Hey, God, does that sound like a good plan?"

Nothing. I knew it was the drugs. I'm able to move some of the smaller pieces off of my chest but I have to be careful, it could be like a house of cards that can come tumbling down. I close my eyes and begin to laugh again. Random childhood memories keep popping into my head. Andy and I would play monopoly for hours. Andy would never let MJ play. Finally, one day she asked why, and Andy told her it was because she was a girl. She walked over, took the corner of the board, and flipped it up into the air. Everything went flying. I was laughing which, of course, made Andy crazy mad. When he asked her why she did it, she said cuz she's a girl and she will keep doing it until we let her play. A couple of weeks later, he told her she could play with us. We lost so badly that we never played that game again.

I'm able to push the stuff on my chest down further so it's easier to breathe. I'm tired. I need to close my eyes.

"Are you sure you want to sleep?"

"Oh, you're back, so I must be losing what little I have left of my mind. I'm very tired."

"The longer you're here, the less of a chance you have to see MJ and Patrick. The choice is yours."

"You give us free will to choose but then when we do, you make us question ourselves. Oh, and before you question what I mean by "we," I'm asking for everyone who's ever questioned why. You know we all have a long list of questions for you. You know questions that question what you where thinking about when you made certain stuff. One really important one is, why did you ever make Roaches, spiders, and mosquitoes?"

No answer . . . just like I thought. I really need to rest, but my teeth are chattering so bad, I want to pull my hair out. I move some stuff around and find a small piece of wood. As disgusting as this is, I can't take the chattering. I put the wood in my mouth, clamp down and close my eyes. Just a few minutes of rest, that's all I'm asking for.

CHAPTER
TWENTY-EIGHT

Gail

I KNOW JACK WASN'T TOO happy about taking me anywhere, but I need to try and help find Fitz. I only hope I'll be able to face his family. We are getting closer to the site and my heart is beating so hard, I can hear the blood pounding in my ears. Jack takes my hand and I nearly jump out of my skin.

"Gail, you don't have to do this. I can turn this car around right now and take you home."

"No. please, I need to do this."

We pull up and when he flashes his badge, we are escorted past the perimeter. I stop and begin to sway. I feel lightheaded and close my eyes for a moment. Finally, Jack puts his arm around my waist to steady me. My tears fill the corners of my eyes and I try to quickly wipe them away. I open my eyes and gasp.

"Jack, it's massive. How do they even know where to begin to dig him out?"

"You told Travis that you were on the west side of the building, so that's where they are focused. They've brought in experts that are trained to find people in collapsed buildings, along with hundreds of volunteers."

I want to see MJ to apologize but I can't find her. Travis spots us and comes running over. "What are you doing here?"

"When I jumped out the window, I made sure I ran in a straight line towards the fence. I made a mental note of what was on the other side of the fence."

I point towards the tower in the distance. "That tower was in front of me as I was running. You need to move the men in a direct line to that tower, Travis!"

He takes off running, yelling for everyone to follow him. That's when I see her bright red hair blowing in the cold wind. I want to go after her but my feet won't move. Jack pulls me into his arms and I begin to cry. Please, Fitz, hang on.

Fitz

I open my eyes and spit out the wood. At least the chattering has stopped. Unfortunately, darkness is taking over and my biggest fear is coming to life . . . bugs. I can handle the occasional rat that keeps popping up, but not the bugs. I feel like they are crawling all over me. I'm trying not to lose what's left of my mind. "God, we really need to talk about your obsession with these bugs. I can understand the bumblebee, not that I like them and all, but they do serve a purpose. But for the love of all that's holy, God, roaches, spiders and mosquitoes! Please, give me a break here."

"If you want it to stop, then help yourself get out of here. I can't do all the work for you."

Great, now my God is getting snarky. "Fine!"

Think, Fitz, think. I feel around and find a pipe. I can't swing it but I can bang it on my chains. Maybe if they are looking for me, they will hear it. I begin banging and I'm actually making some good tunes. I can't help myself and begin singing Chris Young's "Who I Am with You." I'm so off key, but I don't care. It's how I feel. How I've always felt. "*Cuz who I am with you is who I really wanna be.*" It's like Chris was able to reach in to my heart and see what I really feel.

"God, are you still there? I want to go home now. I'm not ready to go to Heaven and I don't think I'm destined to go to Hell . . . please, God. I don't want to leave my family. My son needs me. I'm supposed to be the one to teach him all about life. I want to watch him grow into a man. I can't do that if I'm not there. My family needs me, God, but truth be told, I need them more—*please.*"

"I told you I'm always here. I agree there is still a lot left for you to do. Maybe you should keep singing?"

I can't imagine he likes my singing. I usually sing in the shower or while I'm riding Wanda. My mind instantly goes back to Wanda getting crushed and mangled. My heart is broken, she was everything to me, and now she is nothing but a mangled heap of metal. When I was sad, I rode her. When I needed to escape the nightmares, I rode her. She was always there for me.

He said sing so I'll sing. "Broken Halos" by Chris Stapleton for you Wanda.

I'm tapping and singing but I could swear I hear a dog barking. I wonder if Andy ever decided on a dog for Stella? My mind is all over the place, kind of like that fish in the movie I've watched with Stella at least a dozen times. The barking gets louder and now I can hear someone yelling my name! God, I hope I'm not dreaming. Please don't let this be the drugs.

"Help! I'm here! Help! Please, help me. I'm alive!" I'm listening, hoping they heard me and then I hear her. I would know that voice anywhere.

"Fitz, I'm here. Thank God! Fitz, hang on, baby, we'll get you out. I promise, we are working on getting you out."

"I new she would find me. Thank you, God. For everything, the good and the bad. Oh, and don't forget to work on the bug thing."

I've committed MJ's smile to my memory and nothing Mateo gave me will ever wipe it away. I close my eyes and there she is. Her beautiful face, smiling back at me. I better go back to singing so they don't forget where I am. I love all of Ed Sheeran's music. Right now I'm thinking of my MJ and I can't help but sing "Thinking Out Loud." It's such a beautiful song for such a beautiful lady. I'm trapped, chained, drugged, beaten, and I'm wondering how can one guy be so damn lucky? I'm really tired now, must have been all that singing. I'll close my eyes and while I wait for them, I can't help but replay every moment of my life with her. "I love you, MJ, always and forever more."

MJ

Trying to get him out is proving to be harder then they thought. The engineers pulled the original blueprints for the building. Sal said we can't just dig him out. They have to come at him from different directions. The engineers have to shore it up. I'm intensely listening as he's explaining it to all of us. They have to support the tunnels they are digging or they will collapse in on themselves. Kind of like digging a hole at the beach and the sand keeps sliding back into the hole. If I thought I could get to him faster, I would get down on my knees and dig with my bare hands. Now that they figured out where he is, they have to figure out how the floor fell. The engineers have brought in heavy equipment to help with the debris removal. God, he didn't survive all of this only to be crushed just when we found him.

I'm not good at waiting and staring at the area makes my heart ache for him. "Hang on, Fitz. I'm right here—waiting." I keep yelling it over and over again. I'm not sure he can hear me but that doesn't stop me. I want him to know that he's not alone. As long as I'm still breathing, he'll never be alone. The men and women are working furiously on trying to get to him. None of them are slowing down. I'm so grateful for all of them.

In the corner of my eye, I catch a glimpse of Captain Hart with Gail. I'm surprised she came back here, but then again, unlike Fitz, I'm not dense. I knew the day she came to see him in the hospital that she had feelings for him. I also knew it was one-sided. After that, Fitz and I took our vows for life. It's how we were raised; *till death do us part.* She looks comfortable with Hart. Maybe she has finally decided she should move on. She's heading my way. On one hand, I want to throttle her for getting Fitz into this mess. However, I know my husband and he would never blame her. There are givers and takers in this world and Fitz is a giver. He doesn't know any other way to be. It's part of his quirky charm.

"Hi, Captain . . . Gail."

"MJ, I'm so sorry."

I hold up my hand, stopping her before she can say another word. "Gail, you are not to blame for any of this. Fitz will always try to right the wrongs in the world. I just want to get him out of here and home, where I can take care of him."

She looks to Hart and then back to me, like she has a secret or something. "Look, if you know something you need to tell me now!" My voice a lot louder then I intended.

"He's going to need a lot of medical attention, MJ. He was

drugged and whipped."

My stomach rolls and I'm trying not to panic. "Do you know what they drugged him with?"

Hart's grip on her tightens, which doesn't go unnoticed by me. The captain doesn't give her a chance to answer.

"The feds are questioning Mateo now. Simmons said as soon as he knows, he'll let me know. MJ, he's strong."

I really don't want to hear anymore of this. "Excuse me, I need to get back to the workers that are helping my husband." I walk away. My dad always told me "*Sometimes, Makenna, the less said, the bigger the punch it packs.*" I think this is one of those times. I want to cry but I'm afraid if I do, I'll never stop. I don't want to admit how scared I really am. Lucas helps my dad get his wheelchair close to me. I reach over and take his hand. We don't have to say anything, my dad understands.

Darkness has slowly taken over the day. There are spotlights all around us and some are shining into the hole where Fitz is. It's making it harder to see. Just when I think we are making progress, the workers stop.

"Sal, why are they stopping?!"

He pulls me around the side of the lights, so I can see better. It's a huge hole with a lot of wood piled inside. "We got most of the dirt out. We think he's right under that pile of wood. We need to come at it from the top. That will avoid it collapsing in around him."

They bring in huge cranes and now they are lowering a man into the hole. I'm watching him slowly peel away the layers of wood. In that instant, my heart begins to race. Finally, I see his hand come up connected to a huge chain. My instinct makes me reach out to grab his hand. Sal holds me back. He knows us long enough to know I would do anything to reach him. I watch as they clear away more of the wood and finally, they have full access to him. They quickly cut him away from the chain. Then another rescue worker, with a basket type of stretcher, is lowered down. When they finally have him secured, they lift him to safety. I'm pushing my way through everyone, yelling his name over and over. Finally, I hear him.

"MJ!"

I reach in and he grabs my hand, it's ice cold. I'm running along side the stretcher towards the ambulance. I yell back to Sal. "Take care of my parents."

He just keeps chanting mine and Patrick's name over and over again. "I'm here, babe. You've come this far and fought so hard. Don't give up now—please. I need you, Fitzy!"

He smiles that beautiful smirk that I love so much. "Thank you, God." I whisper, as he is loaded into an ambulance.

The ride to the hospital seems to take forever. I want to take him in my arms and never let him go, but the EMT's are working on him and I'll only be in the way. One minute he's lucid and then next he thinks he's talking to God.

When we finally get there, a team is waiting for us. They quickly take him away and the nurse wants to ask me questions. I know she's just doing her job but I can't focus on anything she is saying. Andy and Sal come running in with my mom and dad. "Andy, thank God you're here. Please answer her questions. I just can't right now." Mom stays with him, offering to help.

I head over towards my dad. I drop to my knees and with my head in his lap, I begin to cry. My dad's trembling fingers try to wipe away my tears. I don't know if I'll be able to stop them or if we'll ever be the same again after this.

CHAPTER
TWENTY-NINE

Hart

T HEY PULLED HIM OUT JUST as the ground underneath him collapsed, taking one of the cranes with it. He survived this far, but now hell for him will really begin. It's going to be very hard on his family watching everything he will be experiencing. I lived through it with my sister. If I didn't have Fitz to turn to, I don't know what I would have done. He's the only one who knew. The only one I reached out to. Every time she would start using again, he would help me pick up the pieces. Unfortunately, the last time she didn't make it. I need to be strong for him and his family just like he was for me. It's the least I can do.

The hospital waiting room is packed. There is a line of supporters to donate blood: police, fire fighters, and everyone from his neighborhood. Good people exist, even in this sick, twisted world we live in. Fitz proves that every day.

There is a lot of tension between Gail and MJ. I know MJ doesn't mean to blame her or anyone, for that matter, she's just protecting her family. My ringing phone snaps me out of my daydream.

"Hey, Simmons, please tell me you have some good news for me."

"Yeah, Mateo, is singing like a canary. He gave up his sister Regina, his uncle Santillana Maximiliano in Colombia, along with his China connection."

"What about the drug he shot Fitz up with? Were you able to find out exactly what it was?"

"He said he gave him pure Fentanyl. He didn't cut it with Heroin like he did for his dealers. He wanted to get Fitz hooked fast and make his life hell. At least now the doctors will know what they are dealing with and can begin the right treatment. Hang in there, Fitz is one stubborn, tough SOB."

"Do you believe him?"

"The deal we made with him hinges on Fitz surviving. So, it's in his best interest to tell the truth."

"Okay, thanks. I'll let the doctors know what they are up against."

I get a hold of one of the nurses and tell her what I found out. The look on her face is grim. However, she said she would pass the information along to the doctor that's treating him.

I promised MJ when I found out, I would let her know. I know it's not good news but I'm glad Pat is with her. She is sitting on the floor with her head in his lap. He's gently running his hand through her hair. I clear my throat and she looks up at me, her eyes are not their usual sparkling green. They are sad, and it breaks my heart.

"I promised you when I found out what they gave him I would let you know. It was pure Fentanyl. I already let the staff know, so they can start the proper treatment." She says nothing, and for a moment I think maybe she didn't hear me. But then, the tears slide down her cheeks. She gets up and crawls onto Pat's lap. She needs her dad and he's doing his best to comfort her. Andy and Annie rush over. They huddle together, and I back away.

MJ

My dad is my rock and I don't know what I would do without him. I know he's scared, yet he's put his fear aside to comfort me. My mind keeps playing back Gail's words "he was whipped and drugged." I know the captain was trying to be positive since he found out what they gave him, like that would make a difference. To the doctors, I'm sure it does. But to me, it doesn't. My husband has been tortured and it's something we all will have to live with for the rest of our lives. It took so long for him to come to terms with everything that happened in his childhood. I didn't find out what happened to him as a child until a few years ago. It was something our family never talked about. Fitz was just another part of our family. Before we got together, he wanted me to know it all. That's when he opened his heart to me. That's when my beautiful, dense husband finally had his *aha* moment. He finally realized he is a good person that we all love and nothing will drive us away. God only knows how he will recover from this. I promised I would love him, stand by him and protect him with all that I am and all that I have. For me, nothing will change that. No matter what they've done to him, he will always be my Fitzy.

Earlier, I called Livy and asked her to bring a few things, along with my son. I need him, and when he's ready, so will Fitz. The doors open, and the kids come running in with Livy, trying to keep up behind them. I quickly dry my tears and open my arms. He leaps. I catch him and we both fall backwards. His laughter fills the room.

Andy scoops up Stella and holds her close. These kids are a reminder of what we are all here fighting for . . .the future.

FITZ

I have never been so cold in my life. I can't seem to get anyone's attention. Why can't they hear me? My teeth begin chattering again. This time, I don't have a piece of wood to stop it. They've cut off my clothes and they are talking about warming me up slowly. *"Hello, people, if you give me some clothes to put on, I wouldn't be so damn cold!"* Why is no one listening to me? I finally get rescued. What good does it do, if no one pays attention to me. *"I want my wife."* She'll know what to do, she always knows. *"Did you hear me? I want my wife, NOW!"* Nothing. I try to move but nothing is happening. Why can't I move? "MJ! MJ! I NEED YOU! MJ!"

"He's coming around. Welcome back, Mr. Rodriguez."

"Cold, MJ, need MJ. Want my wife now!"

"I sent the nurse to get her. Let's try and calm down until she gets here. Can you tell me what you're feeling?"

What I'm feeling? Really? What kind of stupid question is that? Why is it when something major happens, people ask stupid questions? "I'm feeling like a man who just had a building fall down on him. I want my wife now, please." I curl up into a ball because my body feels like one big charley horse. Besides that, no one is of any use to me.

My heart starts racing. She's close, I know it. I look past the doctor and see her running towards me, her beautiful red hair everywhere. She pushes her way past the doctor and climbs into my bed. She pulls me into her arms and I know I'm safe. I'm home.

"I love you, MJ."

"Shhh, I know. I need you to calm down. I'm not going anywhere with out you. You need to cooperate with the doctor. You have to do that for me and for Patrick. We need you, Fitzy."

"I'm sorry. I'm so very sorry."

"Stop with the sorry crap. You have nothing to be sorry for."

She's stroking my head and my teeth aren't chattering anymore. "You're better than a piece of dirty wood." I drift off to sleep, knowing she'll make me whole again.

MJ

He's asleep for now, lying on his side with his head in my lap. The nurse informs me she is going to clean his back with warm water and gentle soap. She looks down at his back and then at me with a somber look. Quickly, she averts her eyes to Fitz's back. Once she finishes, the doctor is able to get a better look. I lean over to look and I sink my teeth into my lip to try and stifle my scream. I realize why she looked at me like that. I've never seen wounds like this up close and personal. Even when I had my club, floggers, cat o'nine tails and switches didn't do anything like what I'm seeing. Those were done for pleasure; these were done for torture. I can't stop my tears.

The doctor steps closer to me and gives my shoulder a gentle squeeze. "I know this looks bad, but we are getting to it early enough. After it's all clean, I'm going to treat it with a topical antibiotic and I'll bandage them. Hopefully, they won't scar."

I look at him and I'm trying not to take my anger out on him. It's not his fault. He's just a man, doing his job. Now if he could only stop the emotional scars Fitz will have to endure, all of us will, for the rest of our lives. "So, what is your plan to treat my husband?"

"He has a mild case of hypothermia. I'm slowly bringing his body temperature up to normal. Besides the topical antibiotic for his back, I want to put him on an oral broad-spectrum antibiotic. I removed two Hillman Spike Concrete Anchors from his right thigh. They were in the Vastus Medialis, which in laymen's terms helps move the knee. Lucky for him, they were not in very deep. I worked in construction during my summers off that's the only reason I knew what they were. I also gave him a Tetanus shot."

I'm trying to absorb all of this. The nurse is finished with his back and pulls the blanket up so I can't see.

"What about the drug he was given? Will he go through detox?"

"I understand he was forcefully given injections of Fentanyl. Some facilities offer a rapid detox from fentanyl. They are given Naltrexone, which is an opiate blocker. I don't believe that would be best for him, and it's dangerous. I want to watch him for a couple of days. He has a lot going for him. He's healthy and has a very low BMI. He's taken good care of his body. We need to make sure the entire drug is flushed from his system. He could experience some of the symptoms that go along with detoxing from Fentanyl, such as muscle pain and cramps, sweating, headache, rapid heart rate, nausea, and vomiting. They are the most common. I understand from his medical records that he's never used drugs. That would probably make him more sensitive to the drug. That could make it easier for him to become addicted. I would like him to follow up with a couple of Narcotics Anonymous meetings. After everything he's been through, I would suggest he also have some counseling. It will be good for the whole family, too. Don't worry, I'll have everything written out for you. I don't expect you to remember all of this. The next forty-eight hours are not going to be easy on him. Once he's lucid, I want to give him something warm to drink."

To say I'm overwhelmed is an understatement.

"I'm going to make an exception and let you stay with him. He seems to know you're here which is keeping him calm."

I cock my head and gave him my best no-chance-in-hell I'm leaving look. He backs up and leaves the room. I know I should be nicer, but it's not easy.

"Excuse me, Mrs. Rodriguez."

I look up and realize the nurse is talking to me. "I'm sorry, I was lost in my thoughts."

She takes my hand in both of hers.

"Your husband is a very special man. I know that God is not ready for him yet. He'll pull through this."

"You know my husband?"

"Yes, my name is Sylvia. Ten years ago, my niece, Tonya, was taken right out of our front yard. She was only seven years old. We were playing and I had to go to the bathroom. When I came back outside she was gone. Your husband was one of the investigators. I blamed myself for leaving her outside. He was very kind to me and he made me understand that it wasn't my fault. He kept his promise and he found Tonya alive, even when everyone doubted him! She's graduating high school this year and plans on becoming an engineer. I'm sure there are a million other 'Tonya's' out there. He's a very special man and it's an honor for me to be here, helping him now when he really needs it."

"Thank you."

She goes about her business, checking all of the machines before she heads out. I hold on to him and gently rub his head. I know how much he loves that. He's smirking. I know he's going to be okay. He has to be.

CHAPTER
THIRTY

Fitz

I OPEN MY EYES TO MJ lying next to me. My head is resting on her boob, and I'm trying to suppress my laugh. I look up. Her eyes are closed but she's smiling. I look back down to her boob and I'm thinking how wonderful it would be to play with them for awhile. I feel a definite stirring in my cock. Nice to know after everything I've been through, it's still working. If I stretch just a little, I can get a lock on her nipple. I start to slowly move.

"Don't even think about it."

I look up and her eyes are open wide. Her smile lights up my world. "I thought you were sleeping."

"I know you did. You gravitate towards my boobs every morning. So, why would today be any different. How are you feeling?"

I lift my blanket a little and I see they finally gave me something to wear. It's one of those stupid hospital gowns. I pull it to the side and show her my cock. "Hey look, I think it's winking at you. Glad it still works."

"Well, praise God for that one."

I try not to laugh as she attempts to cover my cock.

"I have to tell you something. When the building collapsed, I started talking to God."

"Fitz, you always talk to God out loud, around the house."

"Yeah, but, MJ, this time, he talked back!"

She raises only one eyebrow with that look of *yeah right, Fitz, you're telling me some tall tales*. I'm about to explain more but the nurse comes in.

"Good Morning. My shift is over and I figured I would check on you before I go home. I wasn't expecting to see you awake. How are you feeling?"

Why does this woman look so familiar to me? Why can't I place her? MJ gently jabs me in my ribs with her elbow.

"I know you. Where do I know you from? Wait, I never forget a face, don't tell me. I know, I helped you a very long time ago. Your niece was abducted right from her front yard—Sylvia!"

"Yes! You remembered."

"I always remember the happy endings, they help me when things don't turn out well."

"Well, you'll be happy to know Tonya is graduating this year. She plans on becoming an engineer."

"You can't imagine how much knowing that means to me."

"I won't keep you. I'll be back tomorrow. You will be fine, but you must follow the doctor's orders."

"I promise I will."

She leaves, and I'm reminded why I do what I do. I look up at MJ and I see tears dancing along her lashes. I know she would rather I call it quits and do something safe, but I don't know any other way.

"My head is really pounding, and I feel really cold again."

"Close your eyes. I'll get the doctor." She slides out of the bed and makes sure she pulls the covers tight around me. I close my eyes but not before she dims the lights. Hopefully, that will help my headache. I don't want her to leave but I don't want her to see me like this.

MJ

I need to update everyone and now seems like a good time to do it. I know what he's doing, but I don't want to push him to hard. We will have to deal with all of this on his terms. When I get to the waiting room, Patrick is asleep on my dad's lap. Andy's got Stella asleep in his arms. Everyone rushes towards me. I'm trying to keep it together even after I notice Gail is still here. I reach down and pick up Patrick. He stirs a little and quickly falls back to sleep.

"Thank you, everyone, for all your support. He's going to be okay, it's going to take some time. The best thing for him right now is rest. When he's up for visitors, I'll let everyone know. In the meantime, Mom, Dad, why don't you go in and sit with him while Andy and I find the doctor."

That was my polite way of getting rid of everyone. I know they mean well but I know what's best for my husband. "Andy, can you find the doctor and let him know that Fitz is still very cold and he has a very bad headache. I need to talk to Father O'Neil, please."

Thankfully, he doesn't question me. I catch Father O'Neil before he heads out and I ask him to stay. After what Fitz told me, I think maybe he needs to talk to someone. He's always been close to the father. I know he's comfortable with him.

"What can I do for you, Makenna?"

He's one of the few people who uses my full name when they're not mad at me. "I think Fitz might need to talk to you alone. He said some things that didn't make sense to me. I don't want to relay what he said. I'd rather have him tell you directly."

"Okay, when your parents come out, I'll go in to see him."

"Thank you."

Pat

Along the way to Fitz's room, I make a vow with myself that I wouldn't lose it. I need to be strong for my family. I will always be there to support my son in whatever he needs. Hearing Annie gasp and seeing how broken he is, sends my heart into a tailspin. He's asleep, but he's shaking. I look up at my wife and she begins to sway. I grab her around her waist and try to hold her up. Thankfully, the nurse walked in right behind us. She pulled a chair next to the bed and helped Annie into it. I quickly wipe away my tears. He doesn't need to know how scared I am for him. He moves a little and the hospital blanket falls away. The lights are dim but that's when I notice it. He's got the Hello Kitty blanket wrapped around his arms. His arms are so huge I can't imagine how he got it around him. She saved it all these years. I would watch her every night creep down the hallway to the bathroom with her blanket. At first, I thought she was sleeping in there, but I soon realized what she was really doing. I said nothing. It seemed to be what he needed. His eyes slightly open to a squint. I'm sure with his monster headache, any light is painful.

"Mom, Dad, I'll be okay. Please, Mom, don't cry."

He tries to reach his hand out to Annie's, it's shaking so bad. As if on cue, the nurse takes it and checks his IV. Then she takes all of his vitals.

"You're running a fever. It could be from the drug or you could have an infection. You're antibiotics should be kicking in."

I don't know if she's talking to us or out loud to herself. Either way, I don't like what I see.

"Ma'am, I would like to speak to the doctor that is responsible for his care." My tone a little bit more harsh then I would have liked.

"He's been paged. I'll also make him aware of the fever. I promise you, we are doing everything we can to help him."

He's such an imposing man but right now, he's that little boy I rescued all those years ago. When he decided to retire, I was so happy. The job can sour you on the human race, if you let it. He was happy doing PI work. Most of it was cheating spouses and some money laundering. This drug shit—it's bad. When this is over, we are going to have to have a come to Jesus meeting. For now, we wait and pray.

CHAPTER
THIRTY-ONE

Hart

I T WAS QUITE EVIDENT THAT MJ wanted everyone out of there, especially Gail. I know she doesn't mean it but right now, she needs someone to blame. The ride back to her house is very quiet. I look over towards her and she seems to be lost in her thoughts. "MJ is really stressed right now and with everyone asking questions it's too much for her. I wouldn't take it personal."

"I would do the same thing if I was in her shoes. I just pray that all of this doesn't break our friendship."

"In time, talk to her. Right now, the best thing you can do is give them space. Even though he wasn't a drug user, that crap was in his system. His reaction to the drug was magnified because of that. He's lucky he didn't OD on that crap. It's very dangerous stuff and right now, he's in a lot of pain. He's very lucky but still he's going through hell."

"How do you know so much about drug use?"

I pull into her driveway and try to find the courage to talk about my sister. "Four years ago, my baby sister got mixed up with drugs. It was a constant revolving door with rehab. Fitz helped me with her every day for four years. If I couldn't go, Fitz would take my mom to visit her. He would even take my sister to her meetings, always making sure she didn't skip out. Four years of ups and downs. Four years of empty promises. Until finally, one day, she never woke up."

"Oh, Jack, I'm so sorry. I didn't know."

"How could you? The only one I ever told was Fitz. When she died, I felt I hit rock bottom. I started to drink. It started out innocently. I would only drink the neck and shoulders out of the bottle. Then it got worse. I needed to numb my doubts."

"Doubts?"

"Did I do enough? Did I do too much?"

"How did you stop?"

"Fitz and I had a come to Jesus meeting, as he called it. He made me realize I still have a life and I can still do so much good with it. I made a choice to live my life to the fullest." I turn and face her. Maybe this is my moment. "Gail, do you think maybe now it's your time to get a life?" I ask. She looks at me, her eyes are wide and her mouth open. "That didn't exactly come out like I wanted it to." I take her hand in mine and bring it up to my lips. Making my intentions perfectly clear. I'm a smart man and I think I can find some space between a rock and a hard place.

"Jack . . ."

I hold up my hand stopping her. "Look, I know, Gail. Anyone would only have to look at you when he enters the room and your face lights up. However, after everything that's gone down this week, you've got to realize that Fitz and MJ are a lock for life. You can waste what's left of your life dreaming about something that's never going to happen or you can take a chance . . . with me."

"I need time."

"I'll walk you in." I get out and always the gentlemen, open the door and walk her inside.

"Get some rest and I'll be by tomorrow to check on you." I lean down and rest my lips on her forehead. I turn and head back to my car. She doesn't stop me. All I hear is the closing of her door.

I'm driving down the winding roads and mentally beating myself up. I should have told her the way I felt years ago. Maybe it would have made a difference back then for both of us. Instead, here we are, two lonely people, sitting on the sidelines of life.

Gail

I have no idea what I should have said to Jack. Here I thought I hid my feelings so well, and it's anything but. The only one who was clueless was Fitz. Maybe Jack is right, maybe it's time I get a life. Before I decide if I want to move forward with anything, I need to resolve everything in my life. I grab the phone and my keys and head to Bailey's house. I'm hoping she's home.

My house is only five minutes from hers. When I pull up, there's no sign of any security. As I make my way to her front door, the light comes on and she opens the door.

"Oh my God, Gail."

She pulls me into her arms. I loosen her grip. "My ribs are very bruised."

"I'm so sorry. Come inside. I'm sure we both have a lot of questions."

I want to believe that she is innocent in all of this. I want to believe that there is still good people in the world and not all mankind is fucked up.

214

"I do have a lot of questions, starting with Emerson."

We head into the kitchen where Bailey makes us some tea. "Did you know he was alive?"

"Gail, you know me. If nothing else, you know how I am with my children. They are my world. Ask yourself this: would I put them through that?"

"What happens now?"

"I would think he's going to jail for a very long time. I've been cleared by the FBI of any involvement and CPS released my kids; they're upstairs.

"May God forgive me, but for my children's sake, it would have been better if he really was dead. At least they could have some sort of closure. Instead, they will be ridiculed at school. I have no intention on staying here. I just haven't figured out my next move yet."

"What about Megan?"

"Are you ready for this? She's not Emerson's daughter."

I feel the blood drain from my face and I know my mouth is really hanging open now. "Excuse me? She's not his daughter? How did you find this out? How sure are you that it's true?"

"Mateo gave up everything he knew to get a deal and that included everything he did for his sister. He created Justin's fake medical records to give to Emerson."

"That's just cruel. Was Justin aware of all of this?"

"No, he thought the money she was bringing in was from a childhood trust fund. Enough about all of this. I want to hear about you. One of the guards told me you got out and Fitz is in the hospital."

I give her the lowdown on everything that happened in that building. Even the fact that I told Fitz how I felt.

"Did you get the answers you needed?"

"What do you mean?"

"Gail, you've been carrying a torch for this man since the day you met him. You've turned a blind eye to anyone who's shown the slightest interest in you. Now, by no fault of your own, you were outed. Were you expecting him to toss aside his wedding ring and claim his undying love for you?"

"Bailey, I've never known you to be cruel."

"It's not cruel; it's the cold hard facts. You hid your feelings for this man from all of your friends. Did you ever ask yourself why?"

"I think, at first, I never thought I could get a man like Fitz, let alone hang onto him. Then, when he got married, I knew that was it. I would never try to break up a family, so I tried to put him out of my mind."

"If you would have come to me, or any of us we would have helped you get past this. Have you decided what you are going to do next?"

I'm staring into my cold cup of tea as if it contains some magic tealeaves. "Captain Jack Hart told me tonight he has feelings for me and maybe it's time I get a life. Maybe I should take him up on that."

"Maybe you need to take that vacation and finally come to terms with your feelings before you start anything with anyone else. You need to be fair to him."

"Maybe you're right."

"Did you get to see Fitz after they got him out of there?"

I take a moment to push away my guilt that I've built up in my mind for everything he's been through. "No, I went to the hospital but MJ wasn't letting anyone but immediate family in to see him and only for a few minutes."

"Okay, well, eventually, I need to see him. If for nothing else, to apologize for my soon to be ex-husband's behavior."

"So, you'll be filing for a divorce." It's more of a statement than a question.

"Of course, I need to put all of this behind me and start over. You might want to do the same."

"I'm going to head home."

She walks me to the door but not before giving me another gentle hug. I never expected her to be so harsh. Then again, maybe that's exactly what I need.

CHAPTER
THIRTY-TWO

Fitz

I HATE HAVING MY FAMILY here, seeing me like this. I know they understand but I can still see it in their eyes every time they look at me—disappointment. I feel it in myself. I should have fought harder. I saw the tail and I got cocky. I led them on a chase through the neighborhood. I should have called the captain and had him send back up right away. I put everything I hold so dear in jeopardy.

Mom went out with MJ to talk to Father McNeil. My dad has not left my side, even though I've tried to push him away. I'm finding it hard to even look him in the eye.

"Dad, I'm sorry. I know what I did was stupid."

"Why are you apologizing?"

"I've been replaying everything in my head and getting caught was my own damn fault."

He wheels his chair as close as he can get to my bed and takes my hand. I just wish the shaking would finally stop.

"It's normal to replay the events over and over again. Thinking if I only did it this way or that way. In the end you had to make a split second decision and you have to learn to live with it."

"It's easy for you to say I need to live with it, but I don't know how."

His grip on my hand gets really tight. "You think it's easy for me to say live with it? I've replayed my shooting every damn night since it happened. Every night in my imagination, I handle it differently and every night, the outcome is still the same. I'm paralyzed from a bullet in my back. I've learned to live with it. I learned to teach my kids, so they don't end up like me. Think about it honestly; what would you have done differently?"

"I thought maybe I was cocky and I should have called for back-up instead of trying to lead them on a chase through the neighborhood."

"You had a split second to make a decision. Did you ever think that maybe you were trying to shake them because you knew time was running out for Gail? Take a second and put yourself back on that bike. What was going through your head?"

"Tick Tock the clock is ticking. That's what Mateo said. It was all I could think about."

"Maybe now you can stop beating yourself up and work on getting better."

"I'm trying but that crap Mateo gave me has really messed with me."

Mom and MJ come in with coffee and Father McNeil.

"Please say that coffee is for me."

MJ passes one to me and gives me a quick kiss. "The doctor gave the okay. How are you feeling?"

"Getting better little bit at a time. When can I go home?"

My mom backs Dad's chair up and turns him around to leave.

"Say goodbye, Pat, we will come back tomorrow. In the meantime, get some rest."

MJ leans in and gives me another kiss. "Hold on, Mom, I'll walk you guys out."

She follows them out but turns around and winks at me. I knew what she was doing. Guess I'm not that dense after all. She always knows what I need.

"Father McNeil, I'd like to talk to you for a bit, if you have the time."

"I'll always have time for you. What's going on that you feel you need to talk to me?"

"When I was buried, I had a conversation with God."

"You always talk to God, we all do at some point in our lives."

"Yeah but here's the thing . . . he answered me. Loud and clear, just like we are talking now."

If he's surprised, his face sure doesn't show it. "Do you think it happened because you were in survival mode?"

"At first, I attributed it to the junk Mateo was shooting me up with."

"Why do I hear a but coming?"

I laugh. "Because you know me so well." My attempt to sit up makes me wince from the pain.

"I finally asked a lot of the questions I avoided for so long, questions about my mom. I think I can look at it differently now. Not as a six-year-old boy. I think I understand a lot more."

"Maybe now you'll stop blaming yourself. If you can really get to that point in your life, then you'll be able take something good away from all of this. That would truly be a blessing."

My grip on the bedside rails gets a little tighter as my mind races with everything that has happened this past week. "God is the one who told me to keep singing. It's because of him, I was found. That and the fact that, in my heart, I knew MJ was close."

"I'm glad you got the answers you were looking for. He's always with us, Fitz. I know sometimes it doesn't seem like it but he is."

"Well, except for the one about the purpose of bugs." His laugh is hardy. We say a prayer of thanks together and then he leaves.

I'm starting to feel a little bit better. The shaking is slowing down. I just wish the headache would go away.

I must have fallen asleep again. I open my eyes, Andy and MJ are here with the kids. I sit up trying to keep the pressure off of my back. When Patrick sees I'm awake, he starts yelling Da da. MJ puts him in my arms and the beeping of the machine fascinates him. When the blood pressure cuff starts to inflate, he screams with delight. I can't help but laugh.

Stella pulls my toes no doubt to get my attention. "Uncle Fitz, are your boo boo's better now?"

"They are getting better, so don't worry about me."

"Why do you have a kitty blanket?"

I look down and realize MJ must have tucked me in with the Hello Kitty blanket. "It's a special healing blanket that was aunt MJ's. I need you to do me a special favor, can you help Aunt MJ with Patrick while I'm here, please?"

"I will but when you come home, you will have to play dress-up with me."

She's always bargaining with me and she always wins.

"Deal." Her smile is from ear to ear. I'm sure she's plotting what she is going to get me to do.

"Hey, guys, I just want to say I'm sorry for everything I put you through."

"I'm going to go change Patrick. Stella, why don't you come

with me?"

MJ takes Patrick out of my arms and they head out. I know what's coming. We've all been together for too long for me not to know. Andy gets out of his chair and comes closer to the bed.

"Fitz, I asked MJ to give me a few minutes alone with you. You have to know that was like pulling teeth. The three of us have been through a lot together. I know no matter what you both will always be there to support me, and vise a versa. But, I can't deal with all the danger that keeps surrounding you. And in turn, surrounds all of us. I'm not a well man and stress is very bad not just for me but for all of us. I think you need to seriously consider a new line of work. I'll help you figure it out but this shit has got to stop!"

"I'm sorry."

"Stop saying you're sorry and start doing something about it. Find something safe to do. I can't live through that ever again. I'm the one who everyone is usually trying to take care of. Every one of them turned to me, Fitz. It was a lot of pressure being that guy that everyone looks to for help. There is plenty of other stuff you could do. If you need help figuring it out, I'll help."

"Okay, now can you do me a favor?"

"After my big speech, it better not be anything crazy."

I can't help but laugh at him even though I know I shouldn't. "Can you get me a new phone? I lost mine when I was grabbed and I want to make some calls."

"I already did it for you. Against my sister's wishes, I might add."

He pulls a phone out of his back pocket and passes it to me. "She didn't want me to have my phone, why?"

As if on cue MJ and the kids are back.

"I felt you needed to rest. Everything else can wait."

I reach out and pull her close to me. "I get that you're nervous. I get that I scared the crap out of you and everyone else. But, babe, I need to see this through. You know I can't just let it go, not just yet."

At that exact moment, Andy picks Stella up in his arms and begins dancing and singing that damn song. MJ rolls her eyes and now 'let it go' will be stuck in my head for the rest of the day.

"Just promise me you won't over do it."

"I promise I'm just going to make a few calls."

Andy's phone beeps. I'm surprised it's charged. "MJ, Lucas just texted me. He's got your car here and he's taking Mom and Dad home. I'm going to take the kids home with them. Fitz, if you need anything let me know."

Like a whirlwind they head out and MJ crawls into the bed with me. I hold up the Hello Kitty blanket and give her a kiss.

"After all these years, you're still saving me."

"Fitz, I love you."

I know her better than she knows herself. She's got something on her mind. "Now how about you ask me what's been nagging you in that beautiful head of yours."

"I spoke to Travis and he said you got Gail out of the cuffs but you couldn't get yourself out in time. Why?"

"It took me longer to get the wire out of her bra then I thought. When I finally got it out, I was able to release her cuffs and only one of mine. Then Mateo came in to give me another shot. I told Gail to run and don't look back. I knew if she got out of that place, she would tell Travis where I was."

Her face is flushed and her freckles . . . out of control.

"You did the bra thingy with Gail?!"

"Well, seeing that we were the only two people being held there and the fact that I don't wear a bra, yeah."

"Your face was between her boobs?! The only boobs you should be putting your face between are these!"

She's pointing to her boobs and I just want to dive in between them. "Hey, if it makes you feel better, I kept my eyes closed the whole time. That's probably why it took me so long."

In a New York minute, she swings her leg over my hips and now she's straddling me. She has her hands on each side of my head. Careful not to touch any part of me she slowly leans in and kisses me, hard and possessive.

When she slowly releases my lips, I open my eyes and I can see a tear dancing on her bottom lashes. "MJ, what are you so afraid of?"

"What if . . ."

I stop her with another kiss, this one soft. She's never been insecure with us and I'm not sure where this is coming from.

"I need to tell you everything that happened and you need to listen. Not what was done to me cause you can see that for yourself. I need to tell you what happened with Gail. She told me she has feelings for me. She said she's had them since she met me."

She takes a hold of both my hands and her grip is tight. "That's not a surprise, Fitz."

"Well, it was to me."

"So, what did you do?"

"I explained to her that I've only ever loved you. I told her it had nothing to do with her. I also explained to her about my parents. I basically let her down easy. I felt bad I never noticed any of this but you've always been my destiny. She said she came to the hospital the day Mark Chambers shot me to tell me how she felt."

"That's the day you proposed to me."

"Yep, I told her she needs to stop wasting her life on something that's never going to happen. She needs to open herself up to other possibilities."

"How did she take it?"

"I don't know cause Mateo came in and gave me more of that crap. After that, it was the bra thing. MJ, the point is, it doesn't matter. She wouldn't have a snowballs chance in hell of turning my head. No one would. It will always be us. That's what God said it was supposed to be. Even if I would have died in that building, I would have found a way to come back and haunt you."

She leans in and rests her forehead on mine. "I'm pregnant. I found out the morning that Gail was abducted. After that, I figured I would wait till you finished this case. Then everything happened. Fitz, I was really scared. I've never been that scared in my life."

"Did you tell anyone else that you're pregnant?"

"Dad knows. I needed someone to tell and we all know if I would have told Andy we would have seen it on eye-witness news at six."

"Don't be scared anymore. We'll figure all of this out, we always do."

I kiss her again and I know we'll be okay. We just need time.

CHAPTER
THIRTY-THREE

Fitz

I𝐓'𝐒 𝐁𝐄𝐄𝐍 𝐓𝐇𝐑𝐄𝐄 𝐃𝐀𝐘𝐒 𝐀𝐍𝐃 I'm finally starting to feel like my old self again. The doctor released me today. It feels good to finally be in my own home. I am going to follow up with the counseling that he suggested. We got home and I fell asleep the minute my head hit the pillow. I told MJ I was going to close my eyes for five minutes. I look at the clock; it's been three hours.

I head downstairs to see what's going on only to find a note from MJ.

Fitzy,

You looked so peaceful, I didn't have the heart to wake you. Livy and I took the kids to the park and then food shopping. We left Travis in charge.

Love you,

MJ

Livy and Travis are leaving tomorrow. I'm sorry to see them go.

I think other than Andy, Travis is the one man I can relate to. He thinks like me and that, in itself, is scary.

I wander around the house, and I find him in my office on his computer.

"Hey, you're up. Did you see MJ's note?"

"Yes, maybe while they are gone, you can fill me in on everything that went down with the case."

"Sure, but you better sit down cuz this is a crazy one. Let's start with the fact that Emerson is alive."

"Are you fucking kidding me?"

"No. Jake was supposed to put them all in WIP. But then Emerson backed out. He was just going to turn everything over to Mateo and Regina. Jake freaked out and made him a prisoner in a safe room in his basement."

I get up and pull a bottle of water from the mini fridge in my office. "But, what about the letter that he left Bailey?"

"He always felt guilty about the kid. That's why he started fighting with Mateo and Regina. He wanted to confess everything to Bailey. He didn't know what to do, so he went to Jake. Jake is the one who told him to write it all in a letter. He set up Emerson's death. He convinced him that once Bailey found out he was really alive, she would forgive him. They would start over and sail off into the sunset."

"That's crazy. All of this for money?"

"Fitz, here's the kicker to the whole thing. The sex app had members that are high up in our government and foreign governments. CEO's, diplomats—you name it—they used it. What these members didn't know is, Mateo tied them into his drug business. Remember the videos that Emerson mentioned in his letter, well copies of them were given to his China connection, along with his family in Colombia. Blackmail material."

"If these people would spend half their time doing something good with their talents, the world would be a much better place."

He gets up and paces which he does when he's on overload. "The cherry on top of all of this is, Emerson is not the kid's father. Mateo faked all the paperwork."

"What the hell? How much of this did Bailey know?"

"At the time she didn't know any of it. Oh, and Jake killed his wife, Roslyn. A deal was made with Mateo. It was contingent on you surviving. He gave up everyone and everything, including what he injected you with."

"Does Bailey's kids know that their father is alive?"

He finally stops pacing and sits back down by his computer. "Unfortunately, we couldn't keep it from them. Innocent children became victims because of greed. I swear, I think you should have to have a license to have a child."

"How's Gail?" I'm picking at a hole in my jeans, hoping he doesn't ask too many questions.

"I know everything, Fitz. I had questions for her before I could close out the case. It didn't take long for me to put it all together. In your defense, I had no clue, either. So, I guess we are both dense."

For the first time today, I laugh, and it feels good. "I was hoping we could still be friends but now that I know, I can't put my wife in that position. I wouldn't like it if she did it to me. You know, it's a matter of respect."

"You need to think about what's next for you. You can't keep getting yourself into these predicaments."

I toss my empty water bottle across the room and it lands in the trash can. "I wouldn't know what to do with myself. Andy wants to open up a healthy food truck. He wants to park it outside different gyms. Now I ask you, do I look like the kind of guy who could do that?"

Now Travis is the one who's laughing.

"I want to throw something out there for you to think about.

Keep your partnership in the agency but limit the type of cases you take. On top of that, you could be a consultant for me at the FBI."

"Or you could quit the FBI and become another partner in our agency. We could work as a team. If I have someone watching my back, it would be different."

"Shit. Livy would love to live in New York. Damn it, Fitz."

"Think about it. I don't need an answer today." I get up and head towards the window and that's when I see her. I grab on to the window frame and I swear I feel like I'm looking through the window of a time machine. Sitting at the curb is Wanda! She's got a big red bow on top of her and MJ is sitting on her.

"Travis!"

"I was wondering how long it was going to take you. Come on, let's go see her."

I hobble outside as quickly as I can. I can't believe what I'm seeing. My beautiful wife is actually sitting on Weeping Wanda!

"I thought she was gone forever." I want to drop to my knees and worship every inch of her but I know my family will surely have me committed.

"I had her repaired and I drove her over here for you. As much as I have big issues with this damn bike, I love you more. When you're better, you can take her out for a spin."

I take a step closer and gently press my lips to hers. "I have one question for you, did she make your coochie weep?"

She throws her head back and laughs. "What do you think?"

"How did you manage this?"

"Andy did. He made sure he got her back and then brought it to the shop he used to work at. He gave them a picture and told them to bring her back to life."

"I have the best family in the world."

"Okay, now back upstairs. You're supposed to be resting."

We head upstairs and my heart is filled with so much joy. No matter what happens, I know that I'm the luckiest guy in the world. "Thank you, God."

Gail

It's been over a week and I haven't gotten up the nerve to go see Fitz. I know I need to but it's not easy. However, I've finally gotten up enough nerve to talk to Jack. I get off the train and head towards his precinct. It's now or never and when I get inside, I find him behind his desk staring at his computer. When he looks up, he sees me and quickly comes around the desk to greet me. It doesn't feel awkward.

"Gail, it's a pleasure to see you. What brings you to my neck of the woods?"

I want to play this cool but I'm geeky and awkward. I can pretty much say I'm the furthest thing from cool. I reach up and give him a hug. I remember watching an episode of The Big Bang Theory where Leonard counted how many seconds he hugged Penny to determine what the hug meant. I find myself attempting to do that now. "I have a question for you."

He leans on the corner of his desk with his arms crossed. I read someplace that crossed arms is a sign that the person is either insecure or uncertain. Jack is definitely not insecure. "Shoot; you have my undivided attention."

"I decided to take some time off and finally use some of the vacation I stock-piled."

"That's great; you earned it. Where are you going?"

"I'm determined to make it to Paris, and I was wondering if you want to go with me?"

He pulls two chairs over and we both take a seat.

"Why are you asking me to go?"

"I thought maybe we could see where this takes us."

He's quiet for a bit and then he gets up moving his chair back. "Gail, I want you to ask me to go with you because you find me interesting and fun. Not because you need to forget Fitz and your feelings for him."

"I'm sorry if that's what you think I'm doing—I'm not. I've never had any kind of serious relationships, so I'm kind of clueless on how to approach this."

"Well, you're kind of putting the cart before the horse. We could start with a first date and not a trip to Paris."

"Oh, I can do that, but I'm still going on vacation."

He takes my hand and kisses it before he pulls me up and gives me a hug. "How about I pick you up tonight at seven for dinner?"

"That sounds like a good start."

I leave and let him get back to work. I have one more stop before I can finally close this chapter of my life.

I haven't seen Fitz since I jumped out of that window. I should have made it my business to stop by sooner, but I couldn't seem to gather up the courage. With every step up to his front door, my stomach is in knots. I'm about to ring the bell when the buzzer goes off and I let myself in. MJ is there to greet me and when our eyes lock, I know he told her everything.

"Hi, Gail, he's in his office. How are you feeling?"

"Good. How's he doing?"

"Ornery as usual."

"I'm was just making him some tea, would you like a cup?"

"Yes, please." I step into his office and he looks much better then I thought he would.

"Hey, Gail, how are you?"

"I'm fine. The better question is how are you?"

"I've been taking it one day at a time."

Patrick runs into the room and leaps into Fitz's arms. MJ follows behind him with our tea.

"He loves that his daddy is home all day. I'll take him inside with me, so you guys can talk."

"Thank you, MJ. Fitz, did you hear the DEA made dozens of arrests connected to Mateo's drug connection. At least something good has come out of all of this."

"Travis has been keeping me in the loop. Have you gone back to work yet?"

"No, and I don't plan to for awhile. I decided to finally take that vacation to Paris. I asked Jack if he wanted to go with me." I dropped that there to see his reaction. He gave me the typical Fitz smirk.

"Captain Hart?"

"Yes, he was a little surprised. We are going to have dinner tonight to discuss it further."

"I'm sure it will work out for you."

"Have you gone back to work?"

"Not yet, I'm taking the time I need to heal. I went to an open Narcotics Anonymous meeting. Next week I'll start physical therapy on my leg. Slow and steady."

"I saw Wanda's back." At the mention of his bike, his face lights up.

"Yes, MJ and Andy made that happen."

"Well, I better get going. I wanted to see for myself that you're okay. I'm putting everything that happened behind me, and I hope you can too."

We get up and he gives me a quick hug. "Thank you for coming by and good luck with Hart."

I head home, replaying everything that happened today like a slow-motion video. I think it was uncomfortable for me with Fitz because MJ knew how I felt. They say ignorance is bliss, now I understand why.

CHAPTER
THIRTY-FOUR

Gail

I CALLED JACK AND ASKED him to meet me at Ristorante Da Claudio in Glen Cove, instead of picking me up. I've been there before. It's quiet and the food is great. To say I'm nervous would be an understatement. I've never asked a man out, let alone on vacation. At least I have my own car, so if things get weird, I can leave. I get there right on time and he's already seated. I pass on the waiter's suggestion on wine since I'm driving, and I remember what he said about his sister.

"How are your ribs doing?"

"They are much better. I went to see Fitz today. It was the first time I've seen him since everything happened. He looks good."

"I know. I spoke to him today. I think he'll be back to himself in no time. So, Paris. How long are you planning on going?"

"That depends on you."

The waiter picks that moment to interrupt us to take our order. After quickly putting in our order, I steer the conversation back towards Paris.

"Gail, I like you a lot, but I think you know that already. I've wanted to spend time with you and get to know you outside of the office for a very long time. However, I won't be the consolation prize. I deserve better."

"Jack, I closed the book on Fitz. After he finally explained everything to me, I realized that was something that could never be. I would never consider you a consolation prize. I would like to get to know you better but I can't change the past. I can't forget the feelings I had for the man. What I can do, is move on, make a life for myself before it's too late. I'm asking you if you want to be a part of that journey. I don't expect an answer tonight." I pull out my phone and quickly send him a text.

"That's my flight information. If you decide to go, I'll see you on the plane. If you're not there, then I've got my answer. Now, how about we have a great dinner."

The food comes and it's wonderful. Jack proceeds to tell me stories from his childhood. His father was a plumber and he thought his son was going to take over his business. Instead, after serving in the United States Navy, he joined the police and became one of the youngest Captains in Brooklyn. The evening was comfortable and pleasant. We parted ways and Paris was never brought up again. I would think if he had any inclination of going, he would have asked more questions. I head home more determined now that I'm going to have a life.

Fitz

Going to that NA meeting made me realize how lucky I am. Through no fault of my own, I could have ended up in a really bad place. The captain called and he's on his way over. I hope I don't have to look at a case. I'm just not ready to jump back into the game yet. Maybe someday, but not today. I increased my physical therapy determined to get back on Wanda. MJ is back from the store with the captain in tow. Patrick and Stella are running through the rooms with Stella's dog Jacob barking and chasing them. It's mass chaos and it's a wonderful life.

"Hey, Captain, come into my office. At least it's quiet in there."

"Fitz, are you ever going to call me Jack?"

"Nope, you'll always be my captain. Now why don't you take a seat and tell me what's going on."

He sits down and tells me everything that's going on with Gail and him. "So, what are you going to do?"

"Fitz, that's why I'm here. I need advice."

MJ walks in right at the tail end of it with coffee for us. "You're asking him for advice?" She bites her lip trying not to laugh. I take a seat behind my desk and put my feet up.

"Okay, Mrs. smarty-pants, what would you do?"

"MJ, she asked me to go to Paris with her."

"Go! She's not asking you to solve world peace for Christ's sake. It's a vacation. I know you don't want to be second fiddle, but did you ever think that maybe if she got to know you, she would see what a great guy you are? You're a great catch. However, nobody knows that but you. You have no baggage. No kids. No great debt. You have a great mom. You have a beautiful home in the God forsaken woods. Get your head out of your ass and start putting yourself at the front of the line. Now, on that note I need to chase the kids."

She runs out, yelling at Patrick and I can't help but laugh.

"Maybe you should listen to my wife, I know I do."

"If nothing else, coming here keeps life interesting." He gets up and heads towards the door.

"Glad I could help." I shout out as he's walking out the door.

Gail

Tonight's the night I leave for Paris. I haven't heard from Jack since that day at the restaurant. I have no idea if he's coming or if I'll be alone, either way, I decided I want to experience all that life has to offer. I don't want to live just to die. That's not living at all. This time, I don't call for a car to take me to the airport. Bailey offered to take me and I accepted. After all, it's probably the last time I'll see her for a long time. She sold her house, filed for divorce and will be making the move to Dallas. At least she came up with a plan to protect her kids.

I splurged for premium seating. I haven't flown in such a long time I wanted to make sure I was comfortable. I make a quick dash to the ladies room. Not sure how long it will be before I can go again.

The flight is full and I keep staring at the door hoping. With every person that walks through the door that's not him, my heart sinks a little bit more. The flight attendant comes up to me and lets me know she needs to take my drink and prepare the cabin for take-off. That's it; no Jack. At least there is no one next to me.

She still hasn't closed the door and now the captain starts making his announcements. I'm wondering why the flight deck door is still open when Jack steps out of the flight deck and into the main cabin. He's smiling at me and I'm more excited than I ever thought I would be. He takes a seat next to me and I lean in and kiss his cheek.

"I thought you weren't coming."

"I've been here awhile. I was catching up with an old friend."

I'm trying to buckle my seatbelt, but I can't stop staring at him. I can't believe I'm really doing this! He reaches over and buckles my seat belt for me. He tilts my head so his lips can press against mine.

"Let the adventure begin, babe."

As we taxi down the runway, he takes my hand. I will remember this exact moment for the rest of my life. This is when my life began.

EPILOGUE

Fitz

One Year Later

S HEER CHAOS, IT'S THE ONLY way to describe what has been going on around here lately. So many life changes have happened, and they all seem to come at once. After talking to MJ, the captain took the biggest leap of faith I think I've ever seen him do. He turned in his papers and took that flight to Paris with Gail. They ended up staying for six months and before they came home, they were married at night in front of the Eiffel Tower. Once they got out of their own way, it was a whirlwind romance. Gail sold her house, resigned from her job and they moved to the captain's home in Haines Falls. In the summer, they turn their home into a camp for kids.

MJ gave birth to our daughter, Mary Elizabeth. We named her after my mom. Her delivery was nothing like Patrick's. We stayed close to home and did all of the classes. I was prepared to go the distance with this one but MJ had her out in two hours. She has MJ's ginger hair but she has my mom's crystal blue eyes. Patrick calls her sissy pants, which we are all hoping doesn't last long, as he pushes her around the house in her carriage. Stella is over the moon about having another doll to play with. Eventually, we will stop having babies and she will have to play with regular toys like everyone else.

I finally gave in, which everyone knew I would, and we got a dog. I told MJ that Patrick and I were having a father-son bonding day. We went to New York Bully Crew. I mean with a name like that, how could we not go there. We adopted a six-year-old pit bull that was rescued from Puerto Rico. Patrick named him Bacon and they are inseparable. He get's along with everyone and always looks like he's smiling. I swear sometimes I think he's laughing at me.

Today, we are celebrating Hudson's graduation from the police academy. Something none of us are happy about. Sal finally told her that he told me her secret. It's put a wedge between them. No amount of groveling has gotten him out of the doghouse. Dad tried everything he could to talk her out of it. Mom threatened to burn all her clothes while she was at work. No one believed Mom would. In the end, it had to be Hudson's choice.

I've been going to therapy. I feel like I've finally put my guilt about my mother behind me. I know the drugs were messing with my mind, but telling Gail my past and sharing with her my fear was huge for me. How many times do we tell people we're fine when inside we are anything but fine? Even though everyone tells me it was the effect of the drugs, I still believe that it was God whom I was having a conversation with. Telling him that I hated him was so hard, but I needed him to understand the pain that I was living with. I just wish he would work on the bug thing.

I'm back at work, but I'm very selective on the cases I choose to work. Travis is now a partner in our agency. He and I have continued to do consulting work with the FBI. Travis and Livy purchased Mrs. Kravitz's brownstone when she decided to move to Florida. They just found out that Livy is pregnant. Of course, MJ is over the moon about it.

Through great hardship comes love, friendship, hope, and faith. I'll never give up helping those who can't help themselves. Call it my hero complex, or call it whatever you like. All I know is, I'm changing my little part of the world for the better. MJ hung a sign up in my office: "You must be the change you want to see in the world" by Mahatma Gandhi. Those are the words we should all live by.

Until we meet again.

Fitz

A Note from the Author

The American Medical Association and the American Society of Addiction Medicine define addiction as a disease. As a society, we need to come together to help those who have become trapped in the endless cycle of trying to get out of their living hell. There are many agencies that can help. Please know that if you need help, you're not in this alone. The first step is the hardest but it's also the most powerful.

www.na.org/

www.addictioncenter.com

www.recovery.org

www.samhsa.gov/find-help/national-helpline

ACKNOWLEDGEMENTS

Thank you. Two very small words but they pack a punch. I'm very lucky; I have the unconditional support of my family and friends. To that end I would like to extend a very special thank you to Jacquelyn Ayres; you get me and that in itself is priceless.

Wendy Shatwell, not only do you feed my UK shopping addiction, you give great advice and support.

All the girls at Give Me Books, thank you so much for keeping me calm though out this process.

Michelle Roberson, you are always willing to stop everything to help me. And not just with Beta reading; you make the best spreadsheets EVER! They have saved me so many times.

Melissa Kulis, you're a fantastic PA and an even better friend.

To all my fantastic Beta readers: Felicia Griffith, Sandra Timmins, Loraine Oliver, Janett Gomez, and Shell Williams. Knowing that I can always count on everyone to help me polish my manuscript is priceless.

A very special thanks to Stacey Ryan Blake of Champagne Book Design. You make my books come to life.

Julie Mishler, thank you for contributing your beautiful words to Fitz's journey.

You can check out more of Julie's work on her Facebook page.
www.facebook.com/julz.mishler

You can check out her book Words From The Heart on all online retailers listed below..
amzn.to/2KEMped
/www.books2read.com/u/mqD7d3

David Wills, what can I say? It was sheer luck that a photo of you showed up on my timeline. That's when I knew I finally found my Fitz.

To see more of David's work you can check out his Facebook page.
/www.facebook.com/david.wills.9

For my husband Rick, there are no words; you're the total package. You are my more. More then I ever dreamed possible.

Finally, for my son Leif, you are the best of us. You make me believe there is still so much good in this world. I'm proud of the man you've become.

Hugs

OTHER BOOKS

ABOUT THE
AUTHOR

Theresa Sederholt was born and raised in Brooklyn New York. She is a graduate of Campbell University in North Carolina, with a degree in Criminal Justice. Theresa now calls Florida home, with her husband, a professional chef, and her two dogs. Experiencing life first hand is what she does best. Believing she can do anything has put her in many crazy situations. Whether it's babysitting a pig farm or cutting the top off of a mini truck; nothing is ever out of reach. Her list is endless, A to Z. Theresa's beliefs are pretty simple. There isn't a luggage rack on the hearse, and give a girl Nutella and espresso and she can change the world. Theresa enjoys connecting with her fans. She can always be reached through her website at:

www.theresasederholt.com

www.ingramcontent.com/pod-product-compliance
Lightning Source LLC
Chambersburg PA
CBHW071428260626
47170CB00008B/2635